No Turning Back

H. L. Wegley

Romantic Suspense

Cover Design: Samantha Fury
http://www.furycoverdesign.com/

ISBN-13: 978-1-732763616
ISBN-10: 1732763615

Also available in eBook publication

OTHER BOOKS BY H. L. WEGLEY

Against All Enemies Series
1 Voice in the Wilderness
2 Voice of Freedom
3 Chasing Freedom

Pure Genius Series
1 Hide and Seek
2 On the Pineapple Express
3 Moon over Maalaea Bay
4 Triple Threat

Witness Protection Series
1 No Safe Place
2 No True Justice
3 No Turning Back

DEDICATION

This novel, *No Turning Back,* is dedicated to Dr. Caroline Savage who lost her fight with cancer as I began writing this story. She left behind her husband, three children and a legacy of serving God in discipleship ministry and through her writing. I had the privilege of having Caroline edit two of my books. Both became award-winning novels. Heaven is richer and we are poorer ... but only for a little while.

CONTENTS

ACKNOWLEDGMENTS

Thanks to my wife, Babe, for her many suggestions for making *No Turning Back* a better story and for listening to me read her the story three times to catch the awkward wording and logical errors.

Thank you again, Samantha Fury, for turning a stock photo into the Beth Sanchez I envisioned as I wrote my story. Thanks for designing another wonderful book cover.

Our Lord says the days of our life are threescore years and ten. If we are strong enough to reach fourscore years, we can expect labor and sorrow, and then we fly away.

I am well into that decade of labor and sorrow, but I am thankful that God has not made it too burdensome and has left me with words and wits enough to complete another novel.

Finally, I thank my Savior that, when I fly away, I know my destination, and it will certainly be a glad morning.

Do not seek vengeance, but leave it to God's righteous anger, because the Lord says, "I will avenge. I will repay."
Romans 12:19
(paraphrased)

Chapter 1

June 14ᵗʰ, Big Bend National Park, Texas, 6:00 a.m.

Elizabeth Alicia Sanchez stopped on the dusty trail lining the north side of the river.

The Rio Grande flowed out of the shadowy Santa Elena Canyon like a wedge, splitting the desert in two and separating her two worlds and her two lives.

Her group of hikers had moved down the trail toward the canyon, but Elizabeth took a moment to look across the river.

Her seven-year-old world across the river assaulted her with brutal images. Flames lighting the smoke-filled night, the foul air carrying the stench of death. Her stomach roiled and she looked away.

People crossed the turbid Rio Grande for many reasons. Some fled poverty for what they hoped would be a better life. Others crossed it with criminal intent, bringing drugs, horror, and depravity with them.

Elizabeth had crossed the river for amnesty and found it in the nation that had given her freedom, citizenship, an MBA, the opportunity to pursue her dreams.

"I love you, America." She smiled.

"Yeah. Me too." It was the twentysomething guy who had sat near her on the van ride to the trailhead.

How had she not noticed him standing only a few feet away, invading her pers—

"Ms. Sanchez? Elizabeth?"

"Just call me Beth." She adjusted the daypack on her back.

"Alright, Beth. Are you okay? You looked sort of ..." His frown wrinkled a forehead crowning a face that drew her gaze like a magnet.

Girl, it's time to reverse polarity.

She chose not to reply to him. Right now, that was better than either lying or telling the truth. And she also chose to ignore the obnoxious voice in her head, because reversing polarity wasn't something Beth wanted to do.

"Uh ... our guide says if we want to make it to the end of the trail for lunch, we need to go." He waited for her, thumbs hooked in his backpack straps.

What was the name that went with that face? Drew something ... "I'm coming. It's just that this is the first time I've seen the Rio Grande in seven years."

Drew something waved her on and then waited until she came alongside him on this wide portion of the trail. He glanced her way. "Seven years?" His steel-blue eyes looked down from several inches above her head. "So, did you grow up in Texas?"

"No, I—" Her right foot slid on pebbles acting like ball bearings. She tried to shift weight to her other foot, but the sliding jerked to a stop. Her ankle rolled until the bone on the outside hit the ground.

A pulse of pain shot through her ankle and into her lower leg.

She fell forward, headed for a face plant on the trail.

The straps of Beth's pack bit into her shoulders and pulled her upright onto her feet. That placed weight on her right foot and brought another sharp pain, sending the muscles of her lower leg spasming.

An arm slid under her right shoulder and took the weight off her foot.

Beth gritted her teeth but couldn't suppress a small groan.

"We need to take a look at that ankle. Looked to me like you rolled it about ninety degrees."

Before she could protest, Drew scooped up her one hundred and twenty-five pounds, as if he were lifting a small child, then carried her to a waist-high boulder and set her on it.

"Hold it, Hunter!" Drew called out to their guide leading the procession of fifteen hikers. "We've got a sprained ankle here." Drew unslung his pack and dropped to one knee at Beth's feet.

He untied the laces on one of her cross trainers. "You know, if you'd been wearing hiking boots, this wouldn't have happened."

Of all the—"Who are you to be telling me how to dress?"

"I'm the person who's telling you your sprained ankle is swelling. I've seen worse, but this is going to hobble you up for a few days, depending on ..."

"Depending on what?" She managed to force out the words through her clenched teeth.

"Depending on how good of shape you're in." His gaze scanned her from her ankle to her waist, eventually reaching her face. He took his time.

"Are you through with your inventory, Mr. Know-It-All?"

"Yep. All done. And you're in great shape. You'll be hiking again in a few days, but not today." He grinned until he saw the expression on her face.

She was mad because she hurt and even madder that Mr. Know-It-All had lectured her, grinned about it, then checked her out. "You are the most—"

"How bad is it?" Hunter stopped a few feet away, his gaze darting between Beth's ankle and Drew's face.

Drew had her sock off and was running his fingers around the outside of her ankle.

If a doctor had been doing that, it would have seemed appropriate. But a tall, twentysomething man, lean but well-muscled, one who was slightly on the rugged side of handsome, feeling her ankle and lower leg was highly—

"She can't walk on it."

"Would you two quit cutting me off." She glared at both of them.

Hunter raised his eyebrows. "I didn't know we were, Ms. Sanchez."

They had been, but it was her thoughts they were interrupting. What must Drew think after her outburst.

Why do you care?

"I don't." Had she said that out loud?

Drew looked at Hunter and shrugged. "She don't. Hope I didn't just cut her off."

Beth blew out a sharp sigh that sounded more like a growl.

Drew glanced at her then focused on Hunter. "But one thing is certain, she can't walk on that ankle. It's barely six o'clock. You wanted to eat lunch with the group at the far end of the trail. Why don't you take them and go on? I can stay with Ms. Sanch—uh, Beth, until you get back. Her day's ruined anyway after—"

"You can say that again." She looked down the trail toward the canyon. "Don't I have any say about what happens to me?"

"As I was saying, Hunter. I can stay and make her completely miserable until you get back and there's not a thing she can do about it. Then a couple of us guys can grab her arms and legs and drag her down the trail to the van."

Beth stifled the urge to stick her tongue out at Mr. Know-It-All. But he'd already treated her like a child, so she wouldn't justify it by doing something juvenile.

Hunter's eyebrows pinched. "You're staying with her? I'm responsible for the safety of everyone in this group. So I—"

"She'll be safe, Hunter. You know that I'm probably the best person here to ensure that."

Beth looked at Drew and raised her eyebrows. Mr. Know-It-All probably was the best person to stay with her. And he's the one she would have picked, but Beth wasn't about to tell him that.

Hunter dipped his head. "But I'm the one who's sticking his neck out here, Drew. I'm counting on you, bro. I don't want any of your drama or dramatics today. And no fights."

"That depends on Ms. Sanchez." One corner of Drew's mouth turned upward.

She would not take whatever bait he was feeding her.

Hunter looked Beth's way. "Sorry about your boring day, Ms. Sanchez. Guess we'll have to give you a rain check."

Drew chuckled. "Except that when it rains in canyon country, you don't want to be here. See you about two o'clock."

Hunter nodded and trotted down the trail toward the group of hikers standing fifty yards away on the bank of the river.

After Hunter left, Drew remained on one knee studying her ankle.

"You know, Mr. ... uh ... Drew—"

"It's Drew West."

"Mr. West. Staring at a woman's bare ankle was scandalous behavior a few years ago. Do that to a lady and it could get you shot."

"A few years ago? Try a hundred and twenty. Let's keep things in perspective, Ms. Sanchez."

"It's Beth. And, yes, let's keep things in perspective. This is going to be a long, *boring*, sweltering day."

"So, I'm babysitting an optimist."

She opened her mouth to protest.

Drew cut her off. "Sweltering is part of the problem. Your ankle is swelling. We don't have any ice, but we do have the Rio Grande. Thirty minutes in the water then thirty minutes elevated. How about it? There'll be less swelling, and you'll heal faster."

"So you've got my whole boring day planned for me. What do they call men like you? Alpha or beta something-or-others?"

"Not me. I'm just somebody who wants to help and who would jump at the chance to spend a little time with you."

The direct approach. At least he was honest. "And why, pray tell, would you want to spend time with me?"

He cleared his throat. "Besides the obvious reasons ..." His eyes studied her face then stopped on her eyes. "... I'm a writer, and from the little bit you've told me, I think you have a story."

An icy chill shook her shoulders despite the warm early morning sun. She had a story. One no one must know, because then no one could tell the wrong person.

The danger hadn't disappeared. It remained a few hundred miles and a border crossing away. Beth needed to make sure it stayed that way.

"My foot is swelling and starting to throb. Can you help me to the river?" She looked away from his intense, penetrating gaze.

He knew she was changing the subject. But would he drop the subject? If not, this would be an unpleasant day with too many nightmares and too many ghosts. And, at the end of it, he would classify her as rude.

Or psycho.

She squelched the irritating voice inside that had turned even more obnoxious.

"Stand on your good foot. We'll go arms-around-shoulders like two buddies."

"You need to understand something. Girls don't have *buddies*."

"Okay. You can be my buddy, but I won't be yours. I'll just be your crutch while we walk to the river." He paused while she stood. "Too bad we can't sit you in the water, so your leg can be elevated while we're cooling it."

"No way am I sitting in that muddy river. It's probably full of little parasites, parasites that do terrible things to bodily functions." She stood and put her right arm on a shoulder that felt like a rock.

Drew shook his head. "We wouldn't want that out here, would we. Speaking of bodily functions ... the outhouse at the trailhead is a quarter of a—I guess we can cross that bridge when we come to it."

Beth blew out a blast of air to empty her frustration. No facilities was another reason this day would be a disaster. She shook her head and took a step with her left foot.

Drew moved with her and his left arm, like a bar of steel, bore her weight when she raised her left foot.

Thanks to Drew's strength, they walked in tandem to the river at near normal walking speed.

He led her to a flat spot on the bank, where the murky water swirled about a foot below her. He bent down to help her sit.

She lowered her injured ankle into the chilly water and grimaced when it felt like ice on the hot, sensitized skin stretched tight around her puffy ankle.

Drew stood. "Be right back. Watch out for those parasites. I wouldn't want to have to pack you back to the trailhead."

How long would he keep up his string of irritating comments?

Drew ran back and grabbed his pack where he had dropped it beside the boulder.

While her ankle cooled, Beth scanned the wilderness around her. At only a little after 6:00 a.m. in the middle of the Big Bend National Park, this was an isolated area with no one around but the hikers. They were probably a half mile down the trail by now. There had been no other vehicles at the trailhead.

She was alone with Mr. Know-It-All, Drew West. If it wasn't for her throbbing, swollen ankle, she might have enjoyed getting to know him better ... provided he didn't start probing into her past.

The canyon was narrow and magnificent with its towering vertical walls. Morning shadows darkened the depths of the canyon. It would be cool in the canyon all morning. But the heat of the early morning sun provided a precursor to what mid-day would bring, the scorching, West-Texas sun.

Drew returned with his pack and dropped it beside a bush.

Beth studied the vegetation around them. Nothing big enough to be called a tree. "It's too bad we don't have any shade trees."

"These scrubby bushes—we'd have to lie down under them to get any shade."

She shot him a sharp glance. "I hope you're not proposing—"

"No. But you really are paranoid, you know." The look Drew gave her wasn't angry, just weird.

Maybe she *was* being paranoid, or pessimistic. But trust of other people, especially men, was not her strong suit.

"Beth, I've got a small plastic tarp in my pack. Maybe I can use it to give us some shade."

Beth looked up the river into the shadows of the canyon. "Too bad we can't go in there to get—"

She drew a sharp breath when two rubber rafts emerged from the darkness deep inside the canyon and floated into the light at the east end.

Two people in each boat. The bearing and dress of the men in the back of each raft had a familiar, ominous look.

Her heart rate accelerated until she had a driving percussion solo playing in her chest.

Cartel drug runners.

She pulled her foot from the water. "Drew, we need to hide, now."

* * *

Drew saw terror in Beth's wide eyes and his defenses went to high alert, DEFCON 2.

He pushed her pack behind some bushes then scooped up both Beth and his pack and scurried back into the thickest bushes lining the river.

Beth clung to him even after he set her down, out of sight of anyone in the rafts.

"Who are they?"

"Two of the men are cartel drug runners. They also traffic people in several ways. The other two men have no idea what's waiting for them at the end of their trip. But nine times out of ten, it's not good."

The two rafts floated out of the canyon and were now only seventy-five yards upstream.

Drew reached into his pack and fished through one pocket until his hand clamped onto cool steel. He pulled out his Governor. He'd loaded this potent little handgun with Winchester PDX1 Defender shotgun shells, basically a mixture of slugs and ball bearings. This ammo was powerful, but most effective out to only ten yards, about the distance from their hiding place to the river.

"Any idea what guns these guys use?"

"AK-47s. The cartel's weapon of choice." Beth's gaze locked onto his handgun. She gripped his wrist. "No, Drew. You try to take them on with that and we're dead."

"Sorry. I'll have to disagree with you. You don't understand what *'that'* is."

"It's a revolver. A handgun. Drew, I've been with people who—"

It was the second time Beth had avoided revealing something about her past.

"Beth, I trusted you to identify them. You need to trust me to indemnify us."

The wild-eyed look she gave him was short on trust and long on fear.

Drew wanted to hear about Beth's past, especially the part she was reluctant to disclose. But he needed to focus on the source of danger, the two swarthy men each sitting in the back of a raft.

As if on cue, the two men grabbed paddles. They could have given Olympic synchronized swimmers a run for a medal as they paddled in synch toward the river bank. And they paddled toward the spot where Beth had been sitting a few moments ago, a spot ten yards away.

Drew sat on the ground behind the short bush, hunched over to stay out of sight. He leaned toward Beth. "These bushes won't stop their bullets, so be still and—"

A soft rattle nearby turned to a loud buzz.

He turned his head and his gaze locked on the source of the noise. A rattlesnake, coiled and agitated, lay about six feet from his head. Maybe five feet from Beth's.

Though Beth tried to cover her mouth, a sharp cry escaped.

Drew's left hand held his gun, but his right hand had found a two-pound rock. He needed to make his choice before the snake lost all patience.

He couldn't shoot the snake and then shoot two men at their current distance before the men in the boat could unleash their weapons.

Drew launched a short prayer, then he launched the rock. He threw as hard as he could from his sitting position. The stone struck the snake's neck and then drove into its coiled body, knocking it several feet away from them. The viper writhed on the ground for a few seconds, then slithered away toward some rocks.

When Drew looked back toward the river, the rafts bumped against the bank and both cartel men, with packs on their backs, held their AK-47s in a ready position. They had heard Beth and the snake. Now the gunmen were also at DEFCON 2.

The vexing question was, when does it become self-defense if you shoot someone? When you know they will shoot you if they see you? But what if they don't see you and might shoot anyway?

One of the gunmen stepped into the shallow water beside his raft and raised his gun.

Drew's answer about when to shoot came in a flash.

Right now.

He gripped his gun with both hands, sitting in firing position, and squeezed the trigger.

The man about to shoot fell backward onto the raft, nearly turning it over. The pop from the Governor's two-and-a-half-inch shotgun shell echoed off the canyon walls leaving Drew's ears ringing.

Beth's hand on his ankle squeezed with surprising strength, but she kept her head out of his way.

The second gunman now stood on the bank. He fired a burst, mowing down bushes three feet to Drew's left.

Drew pushed Beth's head to the ground to protect her, then shot again.

The second man spun around and fell on the bank, half in and half out of the water. His pack landed on the shore.

Drew must have hit him in the shoulder.

One man floated in the water near the bank. Odds were he was dead.

The two *immigrants* began paddling their rafts for the opposite shore.

Drew let them escape.

He and Beth were in no danger now.

Beth's hand, still gripping his ankle, was trembling.

"It's okay, Beth. Both gunmen are down, and their guns are in the water. One's likely dead. But I need to check out the wounded guy."

"But how did—"

"Let's just say they got on the wrong side of the Governor." He popped open the cylinder and pulled out an empty shotgun shell.

Beth's forehead creased with twin frown lines. "A shotgun?"

"Sort of."

"Don't move. Put your *sort of* shotgun down slowly. *Comprende?*" The raspy voice came from behind them, loud, authoritative, and threatening, hinting that the man would love for Drew to try something.

He wouldn't. Not with Beth beside him.

"*Comprende?*" Impeccable Spanish. The guy could turn his accent on and off at will.

"Yes." Drew laid his gun on the ground.

"Hands on your heads and turn around *despacio*, ever so slowly."

Drew had only turned half way around when Beth gasped. "Suarez. He'll kill me," she whispered.

Suarez? Drew looked up into the barrel of an AK-47 held by a man who looked much like the two gunmen he'd shot.

But this guy had the bearing of a leader, a guy who was used to giving commands.

Raspy voice scanned Beth then swore, part in English, part in Spanish. "Señorita Elizabeth Alicia Sanchez. Patience is one of my virtues. I have been waiting for this moment for seven years. What a pleasant surprise."

"What's he talking about, Beth?"

"Silence. No more talking, Señor. Be still and be quiet while I decide how you will die ... and while I decide how to give Señorita Sanchez the fate she deserves."

Drew glanced Beth's way, and the look he saw on her drawn face was one he'd only seen on an actress's face in some old horror flick right before the madman killed her. But Beth wasn't acting.

"What is your name, Señor?" He pointed his gun at Drew's head.

He tried not to flinch or to glare at the man. "Drew West."

"No. Your name is Drew who-shot-my-baby-brother."

Not good. Was his brother the dead guy or the wounded guy?

"It would be most appropriate for you to pray to your patron saint that Ricardo is not dead. If he is dead, you will die for two days. If he lives, maybe eight hours ... or until I grow weary of your screaming."

If Drew hadn't fully understood the reason for Beth's terror, he did now.

There were some mysteries to unravel here—how this man knew Beth, why he hated her. But Drew needed to study the end of that gun barrel pointed at him and find a second or two when it wasn't pointed at either him or Beth.

In the meantime, Drew needed to appear frightened and subservient. The frightened part wasn't difficult. Feigning subservience, when he wanted to kick the man's head off ... that was another matter.

"Señor and Señorita, keep your hands on your heads and stand up, slowly."

"That's a pretty good trick. Getting up slowly from a sitting position with our hands on our heads."

"You do not listen well, Señor West."

"What do you mean, Mr. uh ..."

"Hector Suarez," Beth said. "CEO of the Del Rio Cartel. The man who murdered my mother and father."

The ugly picture came into focus, raising the stakes to the highest level. If Drew didn't act quickly, they were dead.

"My two prisoners, they are deaf. Silence! The only reason I do not kill you now is I need you to tend to my little brother, Ricardo. See, he moves. Walk to him, slowly."

Suarez jammed his gun barrel into Drew's back, prodding him to walk toward Ricardo who lay moaning and holding his injured shoulder with his good hand.

Beth and Drew walked side-by-side to the edge of the river where Ricardo lay. His eyes were closed now, and his jaw clenched as he panted out his pain.

Drew studied the man's right shoulder. The Winchester PDX1 had damaged the outer third of his shoulder. He needed the bleeding stopped and then needed to see an orthopedic surgeon, or he'd never regain full use of his arm.

Ricardo's rifle was nowhere in sight. He must have dropped it in the river. That meant Drew's only available weapon was his body.

He needed to draw Suarez in close and disable him with one well-placed blow or kick. But he must make sure Suarez's rifle was not pointed at Beth when Drew made his move.

"We've got to stop the bleeding." Drew knelt then looked up at Hector Suarez.

Hector dipped his head and motioned Drew toward Ricardo with the barrel of his rifle. That motion moved the gun barrel upward until it pointed over Drew's head and toward the river.

Drew's right leg exploded into motion, driving a powerful kick into the side of Hector's left knee.

He screamed as his knee bent sideways.

Beth had dropped to the ground to Hector's right.

Drew gripped the barrel of the AK-47 and ripped it from Suarez's hands. "Get away from him, Beth."

She rose and backed away.

Suarez stood on his right leg swearing in Spanish and glaring at Drew.

"Shut up and don't move!" Drew pointed the gun at Hector's mid-section.

Suarez sneered. "No green-behind-the-ears gringo tells Hector Suarez what to do."

"It's wet behind the ears. And anyone who gives up his gun so easily has no right say that to the man who took his gun away. Now down on your stomach and hands behind your back, or I'll shoot your other knee, then maybe a shoulder like I did for Ricardo."

Beth stuck a thumb out toward the Rio Grande. "Drew, the two, uh, immigrants paddled across the river."

"Let them go. They're probably going home. Maybe they've realized illegal entry isn't such a good idea, especially when you go on a Del Rio Cartel cruise."

Hector fell when he tried to lie down using only his one good knee. He stretched out on the ground on the bank where Beth had dangled her foot in the water.

"Don't move, Suarez ... Beth how's that ankle feeling?"

"I can walk on it a little. It doesn't hurt as much."

"Good. I need you to go to the bushes and bring my gun and my pack. We need to make sure the Del Rio CEO sticks around for the next board meeting in District Court."

Beth laid a hand on his shoulder. "Please, Drew, be careful. You don't know what he's capable of." She limped away from the river toward the bushes.

"Right now, he needs to know what I'm capable of." Drew worked the firing mechanism of the AK-47 to produce a metallic click.

Suarez's body stiffened at the sound.

"Drew, Elizabeth! Are you okay?" The voice came from up river and was now accompanied by the sound of running feet.

Drew looked toward the canyon.

Hunter ran down the trail toward them. He came to a sliding stop fifty yards away when he saw the gun and the carnage. "We heard the shots and came back to—"

A splash came from the river.

Drew glanced down.

Hector Suarez was gone.

Drew jumped to the edge of the river and scanned the murky water.

Nothing.

He let his gaze rove over the Rio Grande, mostly downstream.

With a blown knee, Suarez wouldn't be a strong swimmer. Regardless, he would have to come up for air soon.

"You'll never catch him, gringo." The pain-filled voice grunted out the words. Ricardo's eyes were open now.

Beth returned and stopped beside Drew. "He's probably right. Some call him Hector Houdini Suarez. He's escaped from some impossible situations."

Hunter approached them. "Does somebody want to tell me what's going on here? I see a dead man and a wounded man and—what happened to the guy on the ground?"

"Hector Suarez got away," Beth said.

"What the—Suarez? The Del Rio Cartel? You sure?"

"I'm sure. He wants to kill me and would have if Drew hadn't stopped him." She put her hand on his shoulder.

That was the first thing he could remember Beth doing that wasn't done in opposition or as an argument. Maybe Suarez's pain was Drew's gain.

He glanced at Beth then looked down at Ricardo. "Suarez hasn't gotten away yet. I'm going down the river to see if I can spot where he comes up."

Beth's hand slipped down to his arm and gripped it with more strength than a woman should have. "Don't go, Drew. There were two AK-47s in that water where he went in."

"Beth, I blew out the guy's knee. He's not going far, and he couldn't afford to stop and look for a gun in muddy water. We need to tie up Ricardo's free hand and then get some pressure on that shoulder wound to stop the bleeding. Here." He handed Beth his Governor. "Hold this on him and let Hunter do the binding. Ricardo may be hurting, but he's still dangerous. If he tries anything, shoot him. Those three slugs and the ball bearings in the shotgun shells will put an end to anything he tries."

Beth took the gun, looked at Hunter, then back at Drew. Her eyes softened to an expression warmer than any she had shown him since they met this morning.

Maybe she liked guns.

Maybe she likes you, dude.

He doubted that just like he doubted he would find Hector Suarez in this jaunt down the river.

Chapter 2

Beth pointed the Governor at the chest of Ricardo.

Hunter had bound the man securely and then had tied a wadded-up T-shirt over Ricardo's shoulder wound. The crude bandage had stopped most of the bleeding.

She glanced at Drew walking down the river with one of the cartel's AK-47s in his hands. He reminded Beth of her father carrying his gun, patrolling their property. He was her hero and she had loved her father dearly, but not his dreadful decision. That decision had cost her family everything.

The picture of Drew also brought back the vivid memories of the death and destruction, of the loss of everything and everyone.

Her breathing turned to panting. Beth willed it to slow.

When the flashbacks came, she no longer flipped out in a full-fledged panic attack. Thankfully, Beth's faith had helped her overcome the attacks, but not yet the nightmares.

Why did she have such a strong emotional reaction to Drew searching for Hector Suarez? This wasn't the normal concern she would feel for anyone in danger. It was palm-sweating, heart-thumping worry. Did the worry come from Drew's similarities to her father?

Part of her concern might have come from realizing that she hadn't been nice to Drew, the man who helped her when she sprained her ankle, saved her from a deadly rattlesnake bite on her face, and then, like some superhero, had stopped three cartel thugs from killing her.

When Drew took down Suarez, he had accomplished feats not even her father could have done. And Rafael Sanchez had performed some incredible exploits.

Hunter walked her way. "I finished the calls on my satphone. The Border Patrol will be here in about thirty-five minutes. Would you like me to take over covering our friend, Ricardo?" Hunter pointed at Drew's Smith and Wesson in her hand.

"No. But thanks anyway. I'm holding the gun on the brother of the man who murdered my family. So, if Suarez shows himself, he knows I'll have no qualms about killing his little brother."

"I'm so sorry, Beth. I didn't realize all you'd been through. But what are the odds that you'd run into that snake out here in Big Bend National Park?"

"Odds don't matter when God is involved." Beth kicked Ricardo's boot and shook her head when he looked up after trying to slide toward the water.

If he was that stupid, maybe she should have let Ricardo go. If he rolled into the river, he would drown, not escape like his big brother.

Hunter cleared his throat. "How do you know it was God?"

She met Hunter's gaze. "He sent me Drew West. If he hadn't, I'd be dead ... or worse."

Hunter nodded and grinned. "Can I tell Drew what you just said?"

"You do that, Hunter, and the Governor might decide to fill your rear end full of buckshot."

"I see. Wouldn't want my rear looking like his shoulder. Okay. I can keep a secret. But, you know, I've known Drew since were kids in Oregon. Just to let you know, he's a little dense when it comes to anything relational or romantic. You've got to spell things out for him if you want him to know."

"Who said anything about romance?" Hunter could be a shortcut to getting to know Drew with minimal risk. And minimizing risk was a way of life for Beth. It was too good of an opportunity to pass up. "If he's that relationally challenged, he probably hasn't had any serious relationships."

The corner of Hunter's mouth turned up, then turned into a full-fledged grin. "So nobody said anything about romance, huh. There have been serious relationships ... on the part of some women. But not Drew. He's left a trail of frustrated, broken-hearted women."

Drew sounded toxic. Maybe she'd played her cards right by not encouraging him.

Hunter continued. "But I've never seen him react like he has around you."

"Me? Why do you say that?"

"When Drew wants something, he goes after it, whole-hog, relentlessly." Hunter cleared his throat again. "May I speak frankly?"

"Of course. I'm not a school girl, Hunter."

"Uh, yeah. I've noticed. And so has Drew. But it's more than how you ... look. Drew looks deeper than that until he finds what he wants or thinks he needs. I think he's found—"

"Come on. We've only known each other for a few hours. How can you, or even Drew, know—"

"Mark my word. You'll see, Beth. Be prepared, because he's good at storming the castle and taking it."

Beth glanced down river.

Drew sauntered up the river toward them, carrying the rifle in one hand. His eyes laser-focused on her.

Decision time. Was she going to raise the drawbridge or leave it down? If Hunter was right, it might not matter. If Drew thought he wanted her, he might storm Beth's castle to get her.

I'm not sure how I feel about that.

* * *

As nearly as Drew could figure it, Suarez had gone under and swam downstream for at least two-hundred yards to surface out of Drew's sight. Suarez had done that in two minutes with a throbbing, useless knee.

Even going with the current and with two good legs, it would have been impressive. With only one good leg, the man seemed superhuman. But Suarez was only human, or Drew couldn't have disabled the man when he had the drop on Beth and Drew.

He focused on Beth, fifty yards down the trail, still holding the Governor on Ricardo, though Hunter stood nearby. And her gaze seemed locked on Drew, studying him.

Ricardo wiggled in the dirt by the river.

She kicked his foot without looking down.

Alert, intelligent, intense, noble-looking like a Spanish aristocrat, and beautiful in a way that was real and significant. Almost no make-up. That was the Beth he'd observed from the outside.

If he was to keep them both alive through the events that would come rushing at them—interrogation, lawyers, maybe depositions, a trial, probably in federal court—he needed to know Beth on the inside. Know what she wanted and needed. Understand the fears lodged in her heart. Then, when he made his offer, would she accept it?

Drew prayed she would. Otherwise, based on what he'd seen today, he feared for their lives.

Would the warmth still be there after Beth had time to digest all that had transpired in the last hour? He was about to find out.

"Bro, did you see any signs of Suarez downriver?" Hunter circled Beth and approached Drew.

"Nada. Eventually, that made the telltale tingling run up the back of my neck, so I came back while I still could. The way he disappeared—guess it gave me the creeps. What's the word on law enforcement?"

"They're on the way. Border Patrol should get here first ... in about twenty-five minutes."

"Good. But I'm not looking forward to this. It's the first time I've ever killed a person."

Hunter nodded. "But not the first time you ever *shot* a person."

"Hunter, the dude had knocked an old lady down, grabbed her purse and then started kicking her."

"I didn't say he didn't deserve it, bro. Just that you've been through these kinds of questions before."

"Don't worry, Drew. They'll listen to what I have to say." Beth's gaze met his. The warmth he'd seen earlier radiated from her eyes.

Maybe something good could come out of a fun hike gone badly awry.

"Thanks, Beth. Guess I'm a little antsy. I've never talked with Border Patrol before."

"I have. They're easy to reason with. They've got a tough job that you just made a little easier."

Was that a smile on Beth's face? Yes. The first genuine smile she'd given him. She was beautiful without the smile, but now ... wow.

Hunter had noticed too. "Somebody should have warned me about you two. I thought this was a group of fun-loving college students out for an all-day excursion. Someone forgot to tell me about the two drug war vets and the firefight right on the Santa Elena Canyon trail."

"You're getting a little carried away, Hunter."

Drew walked by Hunter and stopped beside Beth. "Did Ricardo give you any trouble?"

"No. But I saved his life." She grinned.

Drew sensed his frown growing. "How so?"

"Ricardo Suarez, brother of Hector Houdini Suarez, was going to try to escape. With one shoulder shot to pieces and the other arm bound, he was about to roll into the river to escape like his big brother."

Drew laughed. "You should have let him. Any guy that dumb can only learn the hard way, by experience."

"I wouldn't have let him drown. Just *almost* drown." Beth laughed too.

"You know nothing about my plans." Ricardo growled the words at them.

The ridicule had gotten to him, so he said something almost as stupid as what he'd almost done before Beth stopped him.

Drew looked down at Ricardo and shook his head. "Tell your plans to the cops. They can use a little humor. It's a tough job trying to stop tough guys like you."

"You ought to know," Beth said.

Ricardo lapsed into Spanish.

The man must be deep into his vile vocabulary. Drew had never heard those words, but he'd seen that expression on the faces of men just before Drew had to fight them.

Ricardo eventually stopped and lay still on the ground, panting out his anger and frustration.

"Beth, would you like to translate that for me?"

She shook her head. "I don't talk like that. Mama would have washed my mouth out with soap."

Hunter pointed to the northeast. "Dust cloud on the road by the trailhead. Cops are here. Remember, Drew, you can't use your Oregon LTC in Texas. There are no agreements."

"But I also have license to carry in Idaho. They have a reciprocity agreement with Texas. Remember? We talked about that when I wanted to bring my gun today, Hunter."

Beth's eyes darted between Drew and Hunter. "Reciprocity, virtuosity, animosity, LTC—what are you two talking about?"

"Whether or not the handgun, stuffed in my pack, was legal. By virtue of my Idaho LTC, it is. So, I didn't shoot anyone with an illegal gun. And everything I did with my gun was in self-defense or defending you from a known drug lord."

"Bro, you don't have to convince us. I agree and will back you up. Beth has the identity of the drug lord covered and—"

"He admitted who he was when he called Drew a green-behind-the-ears gringo," Beth said.

"Green-behind-the-ears?" Hunter shook his head. "He admitted who he was then admitted he was stupid. But, bro, even stupid cartel leaders out here will drive away my business."

"If we tell Border Patrol exactly what happened, you don't have to worry about it reflecting on your business reputation."

"I don't know," Hunter said. "After a firefight with a cartel took place right on the trail where I take my hikers, I may not see any more customers this year. Would you hike here if someone told you what happened today?"

Drew nodded toward the trail, where two heavily armed men in uniform approached about one-hundred yards away, their gazes locked on the scene by the river.

Drew needed to prepare Beth for what was coming and for his proposition. He laid his hand on Beth's shoulder. "Beth, after they sort all this out with the various agencies in the DOJ, we might be presented with some hard choices, choices made even harder because of your history with Suarez and by what I did to him. Remember, we have other options than what they'll offer. I'll help you—whatever you need. We don't have to do—"

"Thanks, Drew. But I can take care of myself. You really storm the castle, don't you?"

If that's the way she felt about his offer to save her life ...

Beth reached for his arm.

He ignored Beth's hand tugging on his arm and continued to turn away, toward the men in green uniforms.

One carried a shotgun and the other an M4. The guy with the shotgun pointed at Ricardo.

Then the two looked at Hunter, Beth, and Drew standing on the riverbank. It seemed that the eyes of both men bored into Drew and the two Border Patrol agents did not look happy.

After Beth's initial response to his offer, Drew felt like those men looked. And he needed someone to take out his frustrations on. He glared at the two men approaching him.

Dude, you'd better cool it, or you'll get locked up with Ricardo.

Chapter 3

The two Border Patrol agents stopped seventy-five yards away.

Drew hooked an arm around Beth's waist and pulled her several steps from Ricardo.

"What are you up to, Drew?"

"Keeping us safe." He laid the AK-47 on the ground then held his Governor by the barrel, using his thumb and forefinger, and laid it beside the rifle.

Drew stood and again hooked Beth's waist.

"So putting an arm around me keeps us safe?" She gave him a corner-of-the-eye glance.

"It does. Two young people in love. Looks innocent. Draws sympathy."

"From their faces, I'm not sure about the sympathy part. And love? Speak for yourself, Mr. West."

"Maybe I was."

"Maybe you were what?"

"Speaking for—uh, I think we should put our hands on our heads. That shotgun is pointed at us."

"Border Patrol! Are you the person who called about a shooting?" The man on the right, the guy with the M4, focused on Drew.

"No. He's about two-hundred yards up the trail with a group of hikers on his Big Bend Canyon excursion. I'm Drew West." It was best not to volunteer information about the shooting until he'd given the shooting some context and identified the cartel men.

"How many weapons are here and where are they?"

"My handgun and that man's AK-47 are on the ground. And there are two AK-47s somewhere in the river."

"Keep your hands on your heads." The man on the right motioned for the man with the shotgun to advance toward them. "Check out their guns, Abbott." The man paused and looked at Ricardo. "What's the status of the guy tied up on the ground?"

"That's Ricardo Suarez, baby brother of Hector Suarez. He's wounded in one shoulder. We stopped the bleeding."

"Suarez's little brother? You sure about that?"

"Certain," Beth said. "Hector came here to pick him up, but Drew took Suarez down and got his gun, then Suarez escaped."

"And who are you? Ricardo's girlfriend?"

"No. She's mine." Drew spoke, forcing more confidence into his voice than he felt.

Beth shot him a sharp glance, then the look in her eyes softened.

"Okay. Drew West's girlfriend, identify yourself."

"I am Elizabeth Sanchez, the woman Suarez wants to kill."

The man with the shotgun turned to face his partner. "All visible guns accounted for. Do you want me to search them, Coy?"

"Just Mr. West."

"Seriously? Not the girl?"

"Abbott, you don't know who she is, do you?"

Abbott shrugged. "Ms. Sanchez, I guess."

"Was your father Rafael Sanchez?"

Beth nodded.

"Then I can understand why Suarez wanted to kill you."

"Coy, you want to explain that to me?"

Coy blew out a sigh. "About eight years ago, Rafael Sanchez organized a militia made up of businessmen and farmers, any Mexicans who had grown tired of being fleeced and intimidated by the Del Rio Cartel—well, any Mexican who had guts enough to fight. With his militia, Sanchez nearly drove the cartel out of Northeastern Mexico. But Suarez regrouped and one night brought an army and killed every militiaman in the town and surrounding countryside. Suarez destroyed their houses, killed their livestock, destroyed all their worldly goods, and killed every member of every family. The Laguna Norte massacre."

Abbott swore then shook his head.

Coy continued. "Suarez killed them all ... except Elizabeth Sanchez. And he believes he's got to avenge every betrayal and every resister, or he will lose power. So, Ms. Sanchez is a burr under his sombrero."

Drew turned toward Beth.

Tears streamed down her cheeks. Had she relived those horrific events as Coy described them?

Drew put his arms around her and she cried softly on his shoulder.

The two border agents stood in silence.

After a few moments, Beth raised her head from Drew's shoulder, wiped her eyes, and focused on Coy. "So now you understand why this happened."

Coy nodded but didn't speak.

Drew looked at the body in the edge of the water, hidden from Coy's view by the river bank. "There's a body by the river. That cartel member had his AK-47 trained on us when I shot him."

Coy blew out a sharp blast of air. "Abbott, call an ambulance. Mr. West, Ms. Sanchez, now let's take this from the top. I want to hear what happened." Coy paused. "But keep in mind that we are federal agents."

Beth gave Drew a puzzled frown.

"He's helping us, Beth. Anything we say that can be disproven, or made to look like a lie, is a crime, and he doesn't even have to warn us. No Miranda rights ... nada."

28

"But he believes us, Drew. Isn't that a good thing?"

"Yes. But he's not the federal prosecutor, the man who can call us liars and then twist our arms to get what he wants. Now, with that in mind, let's answer the man's questions."

Beth and Drew answered Coy's carefully constructed questions. Evidently, the senior Border Patrol agent had a lot of experience pulling facts from witnesses.

Beth proved clever in covering herself when answers to questions had the potential to be misconstrued and to be used against her and Drew.

She was clever, intelligent, incredibly beautiful, tough enough to survive tragedy—his admiration seemed to grow with every new discovery about Elizabeth Sanchez.

After about thirty minutes, the questions for Beth and Drew slowed to a trickle, then they ended.

But Ricardo had refused to answer anything directed at him. His response to each question was to swear at the agents in Spanish.

"Ricardo lies there in pain and swears at the people who control his future," Beth said. She lowered her voice. "In Mexico, we would call him *tonto,* a fool."

"So the Lone Ranger was calling his sidekick, Tonto, a fool?"

"I don't know who you're talking about. But calling his sidekick *tonto* probably made him angry. What did he call the Lone Ranger?"

"Kemosabe."

"Did you say *quien no sabe?*"

"Maybe. It sounds sorta' like what I said."

"Then they must have argued a lot."

"Argued?"

"Drew, *quien no sabe* means a person who has no understanding. You know, stupid, idiotic, a moron."

"As a kid, I enjoyed watching those old Lone Ranger and Tonto reruns. I had no idea they had such a toxic relationship." Drew grinned then looked down the trail at the two paramedics headed toward them carrying a stretcher. "Hey, Ricardo, here comes your ride to the hospital. What would you do if one of those guys called you kemosabe?"

"I kill them, just like I do to you one day." He growled out the words through clenched teeth.

"Now that's what I call a toxic relationship." Drew stepped off the trail to let the paramedics pass.

They set the stretcher on the ground and unslung their packs. One of them, with a small container in his hand, approached Ricardo.

He swore at the man and turned his head away.

"I was going to give you something for pain," the paramedic said. "I'll just note that you refused it."

Ricardo turned back and opened his mouth to speak.

The paramedic turned away and put the container back in his pack.

Drew leaned close to Beth. "You're right about Ricardo. I hope Hector does hand the cartel over to him. It won't last long with Tonto holding the reins."

"Suarez won't give control to Ricardo. It is the family bond Mexicans have that makes Hector say this, but it will never happen."

"Well it sure won't happen with Ricardo in prison."

"But you and I have to put him there, Drew."

"That's a discussion we need to have with Coy. They're not going to just turn us loose. There will be a grand jury then, if Ricardo's indicted, a trial. All of that happens in a federal court somewhere in Texas."

"We won't be safe in Texas, especially if we're going to testify to the grand jury. Suarez will send people to kill us." She gripped Drew's arm. "He won't stop coming after us unless he's dead ... or until we are. He sent a whole army to my town."

"I've got a plan, Beth."

"To kill Suarez?"

"Not exactly, but that could be accommodated."

"You're as crazy as Ricardo if you're thinking of taking on Hector and the Del Rio Cartel."

"I'm thinking about keeping you safe. But let's talk to Coy before—"

"Am I going to like this plan, Drew?" Beth's eyes studied his, searching for an answer. She didn't look alarmed or angry.

"I hope so. Because I don't think you'll care for any of the alternatives, including what the prosecutor offers."

Her eyes said she'd settled on an answer to her question. Her conclusion seemed to be that Drew West was full of it.

But Drew could change her mind. He'd always been able to change people's minds. Most often by pounding that person into submission. Or letting them watch while he did that to someone else. If blowing out Suarez's knee hadn't been enough for Beth, maybe he needed to take a different approach with her.

Other law enforcement officers arrived, ending the discussion of Drew's plan and leaving him in a quandary.

From the bits and pieces of conversation Drew gleaned from the officers, it sounded like one was a Brewster County Deputy Sheriff and another a DEA agent stationed in Pecos.

The third man, the tall, quiet one, remained a mystery. Maybe he was from the FBI.

Drew took Beth's hand and pulled her toward Coy.

The Border Patrol agent sounded like he was wrapping up a discussion with the DEA agent.

Coy turned toward Beth and Drew. "I'll bet you two have some questions about your future."

"How did you know?" Drew said. "A lucky guess?"

"You and Ms. Sanchez are pretty sharp or you couldn't have taken down Suarez. So you've probably deduced that there is a federal court case in your future."

Drew nodded. "If we testify, there—"

"No, Drew. *When* we testify."

Coy smiled. "I like that kind of talk."

"Okay." Drew looked down at Beth. "*When* we testify." He turned toward Coy. "Where will this take place and what protection will we have? Suarez will come after us for a lot of reasons. But the personal reasons are the most concerning."

"Yeah." Coy blew out a breath. "The center of this activity will be US District Court in Pecos."

"Seriously? Pecos?" Drew said. "Isn't that in the middle of nowhere?"

"Want my advice? Don't say that to the judge."

Drew nodded. "Point taken."

Coy continued. "The first item of business in Pecos will be a grand jury then, most likely, the trial. And I know for a fact that the prosecutors in Pecos will go hard after the Del Rio Cartel, trying to damage it as much as possible."

"But will they prevent Suarez from damaging Beth and me?"

"We'll have to talk to the prosecutor about that. And, these days, you never know what the DOJ has up its sleeve. Come on, you two. Get your things ... well, whatever we haven't confiscated as evidence. We're taking you to Pecos."

Beth's gaze dropped to the ground. She stared at the sandy soil with a blank expression that didn't belong on such a perfectly sculpted face. "So, it begins." She looked up at Drew, with those searching eyes. "I may never make it out of this alive."

"Yes, you will, Beth. I'll see to that, no matter what it takes."

Her eyes widened. "No matter what? That covers a lot of possibilities from dangerous to deadly."

"I realize that you hardly know me. But I promise you this ... before Suarez can get close enough to hurt you, I'll kill him, Beth. *No matter what.*"

Chapter 4

Beth did not trust the federal prosecutor.

Dana Whittaker, the man who would oversee Ricardo's prosecution, leaned back in his office chair, thumbs hooked in the pockets of his suit pants. "So, that's the plan. Any questions?"

She had seen men like him, anxious to move up the ladder in their organization. Putting away members of the cartel was a feather Mr. Whittaker wanted in his cap more than any concern he had for Drew and her.

Beth tried to stare the man down, but the intensity of his eyes matched hers, and he refused to blink.

She broke eye contact with him. "The DOJ is going to force us into some old ranch house around here and use it as a safe house until you get an indictment on Ricardo, aren't they?"

"Ms. Sanchez, do I detect a lack of appreciation for what we're doing for you? And we're not forcing you to do anything except comply with a subpoena to testify after we convene the grand jury."

Drew plopped his hand on the prosecutor's desk. "A subpoena to testify. That means we're free to go, right?"

"Yes. You have that right. But if you leave without our protection, you won't live to testify against the little brother of Hector Suarez."

"Beth," Drew cupped her chin and lifted her head until she looked up into his steel blue eyes. "Do you trust me?"

The look in his eyes was wild and fierce, but also exhilarating.

No. Those eyes are downright scary.

Regardless of what the little voice inside Beth said, those eyes attracted her like no other eyes ever had. "You saved my life, Drew. Two or three times. Yes, I trust you."

"Hold it, Mr. West. You have no ability—"

Drew shoved a Palm at Whittaker. "I can keep you safe, Beth. I know how to do that. Come with me to a place this guy doesn't need to know about, and Suarez won't be able to find."

"Ms. Sanchez, you need my—our protection. Don't listen to this—this—"

"This what?" Drew whirled and grabbed a fistful of Whittaker's dress shirt. "You don't know me from Adam, Mr. Prosecutor. And you have no idea what I'm capable of."

"If you don't take your hands off me, you'll see what I—what the law is capable of."

Drew released the wad of wrinkled white shirt he'd used to pull the man out of his chair and onto his feet.

Whittaker looked down and tried to rub the wrinkles from his shirt. He didn't reply.

Beth looked up at Drew. He was powerful. She had felt those arms of steel. Drew was a skilled fighter, as Beth had seen. But could he stop a professional killer like Hector Suarez?

His eyes said he could. Said he wanted to.

Beth looked at Whittaker, then back at Drew.

No comparison.

"I'll go with you, Drew. Let's get out of here."

Drew waved at Whittaker. "See you when the grand jury convenes. A day or two before if you need to go over things with us."

"But—but how do I contact you? How can—"

"Call Hunter Jones, Big Bend Excursions. He'll know how to reach me."

Beth pulled Drew out the door of the prosecutor's office. "You take too many chances. He could have you arrested for assault, you know."

"Nah. To satisfy him, I'd just promise to send his shirt to the cleaners. You never have to take men like Whittaker to the cleaners, physically, because the only place they'll fight you is in a courtroom."

In the hallway, a man approaching called out to them. "Mr. West, Ms. Sanchez, may I have a word with you?"

Beth recognized him. The tall, mysterious man who wasn't with the DEA, Border Patrol, or the Brewster County Sheriff's Department. "Drew, maybe we should hear what he has to say."

"Yeah. Whatever it is, it's got to be better than Whittaker's suggestion."

The tall man stopped in front of them. "I'm Special Agent Tom Preston, FBI. I happened to be in this area and heard about the call for help and then heard Suarez's name. You turned down Whittaker's offer for protection, didn't you?"

"Yeah." Drew said. "We didn't want to be cooped up in some house in this area with Suarez and his army trying to get us."

"I've seen what he can do, Agent Preston," Beth took Drew's hand.

"Yes. You have." Preston said. "More than any of us here in Pecos."

"And Drew has already saved my life several times."

Preston nodded. "What I came to tell you is that I'll keep a close watch on info coming from our Intelligence Branch. They're pretty good at tracking cartel movements across our borders. If I see anything you should know, how can I contact you?"

"I'll tell Hunter Jones, the tour guide, you might be calling him." Drew pulled out his wallet and fished out a business card. "Here's Hunter's number. You can reach him twenty-four-seven and he'll always be able to reach me."

"Cautious. That's good." Preston turned to Beth. "You've hooked up with a good man, Ms. Sanchez. You two take care." Preston shook their hands and walked away down the hall.

"Hooked up? Drew, what did he mean by—"

"It's just an expression. He didn't mean what you're thinking."

"Then I hope he *did* mean what *you're* thinking."

"Beth, regardless of what I'm thinking or not thinking, you're safe with me."

"Here's something for *you* to think about. I'm going to hold you to that, Drew."

There was a lot to this hooking-up-with-Drew arrangement that, due to the threats and danger from Suarez, Beth hadn't carefully thought through. The best she could do, for now, was to address each issue as it arose and pray that she could handle each one.

But one concern that she hadn't been able to handle was the sway that Drew West had over her thoughts and decisions. Beth had that research scientist personality type, the type that used evidence and rationality to make sense of things and then, and only then, would she make decisions.

How in heaven's name had she been so easily persuaded to place her life in the hands of a near stranger? It seemed that Drew had short-circuited her decision-making process. So did that make him a danger to Beth Sanchez?

I don't want to think about that right now.

Beth led Drew out of the federal building and into the scorching afternoon sun. She looked at the cars along the wide street, then she drew a sharp breath. "We don't have a car. How are we getting—"

"There he is." Drew pointed across the street to the large van in front of the Brewster County Courthouse, directly across from the federal courthouse. "Hunter almost flunked civics in high school. Keeps confusing country with county. Maybe spelling was his real problem."

"Mr. West, I'm beginning to think you are full of you know what."

"I see I'm coming up in the world—well, in your estimation. The first time I mentioned having a plan for us, you acted like you *knew* I was full of it."

Hunter slid out of the van and waved at them.

The engine was running. That meant the van would be cool, a good place to relax and think through what was coming. How far had Drew thought his plan through? Was he the spontaneous type who never bothered to—

Beth realized her hand was in Drew's and he had just squeezed it.

"Bet you're wondering how we're going to get your things and slip out of Texas unnoticed. Right?"

She squeezed back. "So what are you really, Drew West? A musclebound psychic?"

"This is going to be fun. Not a dull moment with you around. So what are you really, Beth Sanchez? One of those mysterious, play-hard-to-get women? INTJ or is it K? Never did understand that Meyers-Briggs stuff when I took psychology."

Drew knew her personality type. This was uncanny, weird. Like a dozen other things about Drew West. But, despite their precarious situation, it was weird in a nice sort of way.

As they climbed into Hunter's van, a song played in Beth's mind. It was on repeat. That Wizard of Oz song about being off to see the wizard. But she didn't need to travel to see him. The wizard had just sat down beside her in the van.

And Beth Sanchez was not clicking red heels, because she wasn't going home. She was going somewhere that Mr. Whittaker didn't need to know about—wherever that was.

Chapter 5

Hector Suarez sat on the examining table and grimaced as the sixty-something man in a white coat flexed Hector's throbbing knee.

"Fix it, doctor."

"I can do that, Mr. Suarez, if you've got the patience. But I do not think—"

"Define patience, Señor."

"We can do the surgery later this week. After four months of rehab, you'll be walking fine on it. But, at your age, it will take about eight or nine months to get your knee back to full strength."

"For the surgery, I will be unconscious, no?"

"Nearly so. Heavily sedated."

"Then there will be no surgery. I must never be unconscious or defenseless. And I do not have four months to wait before I am 'walking fine'."

The doctor cleared his throat. "When do you need to walk on it?"

"Tomorrow."

"But, Mr. Suarez—"

"It's *El Capitan* to you."

"Yes, uh, *El Capitan*. But tomorrow is impossible."

"Then you must find a way to make it possible, or I will find a way to end your medical practice, permanently." Suarez pulled his Glock from behind his back and studied the doctor's eyes. Persuasion came in all sizes, but nine millimeters seemed to be the most effective.

The man's eyes widened, and one hand went to his throat.

"You look like you have found a way for me to walk on this knee tomorrow."

The doctor nodded.

"So, tell me about my medical miracle that will have me walking on this knee by tomorrow."

"I do not recommend this, because you might damage the knee further by—"

"No, Señor. I want a medical miracle that will not cause further damage to my knee but allows me to walk on it tomorrow."

"*Si, El Capitan.* I will fit you with a knee brace, so you can walk without hurting it. Then I will give you a shot, a strong steroid, and some pain medication. But in two or three days, your knee—"

"What if I need to walk on it for two or three days due to unexpected circumstances?"

"I can give you more steroids, oral steroids. They will likely give you indigestion and interfere with your sleep."

"That is not a concern. It will be my medical miracle. How long do I have to wait for this miraculous event?"

"I'll need fifteen minutes to find the right brace and adjust it. A few more minutes to shoot up your knee, and then you can pick up the prescriptions on your way out, *El Capitan*. About thirty minutes total."

Suarez nodded. "Shooting up my knee ... it is much better than shooting up you, *si*?"

The doctor wiped his forehead with a handkerchief as he left the room to get the brace and prepare the injection.

Suarez had handled the doctor well and got what he needed. Now for his other needs.

He pulled out his secure cell and hit Ramon's entry on his contact list. His most trusted detective answered on the second ring.

"Ramon, what did you find out in Pecos?"

"My sources say calls and e-mails went out to a large pool for a grand jury. They expect it to convene in a few weeks."

"They are trying to push Ricardo's conviction through quickly. I anticipated them taking several months."

"It seems this prosecutor is trying to make a name for himself."

"What's his name?"

"Whittaker. Rumor has it that he doesn't like you, Hector."

"Then I will give him more reasons not to like me. Perhaps his witnesses will all disappear. Did you find out where this Drew West lives?"

"It appears that he rented a room at a Holiday Inn and Suites here in Texas, but he's from Oregon."

"Oregon? How do you know that, Ramon?"

"It appears that he rented the room under his business name. I looked it up in an online business name database. The name is registered in Oregon with Señor West as the owner. But the physical address was not in the database."

"Keep looking. And Señorita Sanchez?"

"According to the university, she was living in Bryan, Texas with a relative. But she left Pecos with Señor West. We'll have to see where she turns up."

"I cannot believe that they did not accept witness protection." Either they were fools or much smarter than Suarez anticipated. "So we will not be breaching a safe house tomorrow?"

"You mean breach, as in blow up?"

Suarez didn't reply.

"I think they are trying to hide and protect themselves. We can always get them when they come to Pecos to testify."

"No, Ramon. Those two will stay together somewhere. I know this because I saw them." He'd seen the look of gratefulness and trust in Señorita Sanchez's eyes when she looked at Mr. West. "You will find them. And I will kill them before the grand jury can indict Ricardo. I gave my word to my little brother, so I suggest you start your search now. I will remove all restrictions on your credit card and on the methods you may use. Find them, Ramon!"

As long as she remained alive, Elizabeth Sanchez would remain the single blight on his reputation—a living testimony that his power was not as great as Suarez claimed.

Some foolish farmer would raise Elizabeth Sanchez's banner high and start another militia that would cost Hector hundreds of hours of his time, millions of dollars in revenue, many gray hairs, too much blood and sweat, but never any tears.

Hector's weeping had turned to wrath many years ago. He would kill the militia and their families, as he had before. But that could all be circumvented if he made Señorita Sanchez a supreme example of what happens to people who oppose Hector Suarez—an example by the way he made her die, or the way he forced her to live. He was not sure which it would be, except it would be the one she feared most.

Chapter 6

"Does Suarez know where you live, Beth?"

"I think a more important question, for now, is does he know where *you* live?" She scanned the living room of his suite at the Holiday Inn as if something dreadful lived in some corner of the room or behind a piece of furniture.

Hopefully, it wasn't him that Beth feared.

Drew tried to put himself in her place—agreeing to go with someone she hardly knew and spending the night in Fort Stockton with him. Not many young women of character would do that. But not many such young women had been targeted by the leader of a drug cartel.

He needed to set Beth's mind at ease.

"You can have the bedroom. The couch makes a bed in the living room. I'll take it. We'll be safe for tonight. I rented this room a couple of days ago. When I did, I used my business charge card so, even if Suarez has friends who can access charge card information, he won't find this room unless he knows the name of my writing business. That's not likely."

Beth peered into his eyes with a look of concern in hers. "I've never done anything like this—I mean, spend the night with a guy, unchaperoned."

He grinned. "I have. Hunter and I used to do this all the time."

Beth grabbed a couch pillow and swung it down on his head.

Good thing it was soft. Beth was strong, and she had held nothing back.

When he looked up, she had an enigmatic smile on her full lips. "Do you always do that?"

"Do what?"

"Evade the real question?"

"Whenever I can. Especially when it aggravates a pretty girl."

"Drew, I don't think this is—"

"No, Beth. It is a good idea. And no, I've never done this before either, with or without a chaperone. But it was already nine o'clock when Hunter dropped us off. Now, I've answered your questions. You need to answer mine. Does Suarez know where you live, wherever that is?"

"One more question first."

"Beth?"

"Please." Her expression softened, especially the look in her eyes, an obviously feigned look of vulnerability. Then she laid her hand on his arm. "For my peace of mind."

Evidently, she wasn't above a little manipulation. But, even knowing that, how could he refuse those eyes. "Okay, one more question."

Like with the flip of a switch, the look on Beth's face morphed back to one of concern. "You're in your late twenties. Why haven't you ever been in a situation like this with a member of the opposite sex?"

"Because it's wrong."

"Who says?"

"God says, and I believe Him."

"Then why are you doing it with me?"

"Because I promised Him that I would protect you, no matter what. And this is what 'no matter what' requires right now."

She gave him a weak smile, maybe on the coy side of weak. "That's good to know. I suspected as much, but you should've told me. You're not ashamed of your faith are you, Drew?"

"Ashamed? Of course not. Are you ashamed of being Catholic?"

"If I was, I wouldn't be ashamed of it. But I'm just a non-denominational, evangelical Christ follower."

"But I thought everybody in—"

"Then you thought wrong. The face of Christianity has changed in Mexico over the past thirty years." She paused. "Well, I feel better now about doing something that's wrong."

"But we're not doing anything wrong, Beth."

"You said we were."

"It's wrong in the sense that people shouldn't do things that have an appearance of evil or that tempt them to do wrong."

"So I'm a temptation to you?"

Was she baiting him? "Beth, you are a *frustration* to me."

"You didn't answer my question." Her eyes narrowed until her dark eyebrows nearly touched.

Drew had never seen a woman with the kind of beauty Beth possessed. Any red-blooded male would be attracted to her. Being alone as they were, was a big temptation, even though Drew had vowed not to cross certain lines with a woman until he was married. "Yeah. You're a temptation." He blew out his frustration and a sharp blast of air. "Now, why this line of questioning?"

"If you were me, wouldn't you want to know? We're going to be spending a lot of time together until this thing with Suarez is over. So, I needed to know."

"Are you satisfied, Beth? Because I'm not going any deeper into that subject." He shook his head. "Women would be shocked if they could read men's minds." Had he said that or just thought it?

She smirked. "Maybe you should shock me."

He hit her head with a couch pillow, his blow only slightly softer than her blow to his head.

"My momma warned me about guys like you. Beta males who turn into abusers at the slightest provocation."

"It's alpha males, but I'm not one of them. And you are not the *slightest* provocation, Beth. You are the most—" He gripped her shoulders.

Their eyes met.

Beth drew a sharp breath.

At that moment, the urge to kiss her leaped up from somewhere deep inside. The look in her eyes said she would let him even though she thought it wasn't a good idea.

Temptation had snuck up on them and it stared them in the face.

How was he supposed to deal with it? The Bible said flee temptation. But how could he flee temptation without fleeing Beth?

He had no good answer, so Drew pulled her closer, slipped his arms around her and held her. "I'll keep you safe, Beth. No matter what ... safe in every way."

"I believe you will, Drew West." Her words came wrapped in a hoarse whisper. She looked up at him. "Didn't you have a question to ask me?"

"Yeah..." he tried to rewind the conversation to the question that preceded it, but with Beth's luminous brown eyes so close, the rewind button didn't seem to be working.

Since he couldn't do what he wanted, but needed to do something, Drew kissed her forehead. It was sweet and salty from their day in the desert. A day he would never forget.

She relaxed against him. "Drew ... the question?"

What he needed, but didn't have, was a switch that could toggle Drew West between Beth Sanchez mode and Drew's paranoid protective mode. Without the switch, Drew's distraction could get them killed.

Switch or no switch, you'd better flip something, dude.

For once, Drew appreciated the obnoxious voice inside that usually taunted him.

Where was he? "I was asking where you live, and if you think Suarez knows."

Beth's relaxed body stiffened, and she stepped back from Drew. "For the past seven years, he didn't know where I was, or I would be dead. But after today, he will quickly learn."

"So where do you live?"

"Bryan, Texas. Not far from Texas A&M University. I live with a distant relative."

"How will Suarez 'quickly learn' of this?"

"He has ways. He owns people in positions of responsibility. And he has money to bribe others."

"That means we need to sneak in, get your things, and get out quickly."

"What about my relatives? I need to tell them something."

"Only if you can do it in a way that won't link you to them."

"Drew, eventually, Suarez will learn where I was staying."

"But we can't allow him to know more than that and neither can your relatives. Knowing too much will endanger them."

"We'll be in College Station tomorrow. What if I called them from my department at Texas A&M? I'll tell them I'm out interviewing for jobs."

"You'll need to tell them a little more than that, so they don't report you as missing after a few days. We don't want both the police and Suarez trying to find you. Also, we'll need to rendezvous with your relatives to get your things. So, I guess you'll have to give them a list of what you want, and you'll have to reveal a little about the danger you're in.

Maybe you can tell them that you're being protected. Let me think it through a little more."

"Can I think it through too? After all, I know them."

"Who exactly is *them*?"

"My aunt's cousin, Sophia. Her kids are grown, so she took me in and treated me like a daughter."

"Yeah. Guess you do need to tell her something, but not enough to endanger her."

"And here's how we can do that." Beth pulled him to the living room couch, then sat.

Drew sat beside her. When he looked down at his side, her hand was in his. It seemed natural. His hand, curled around hers, seemed to have found its home.

He and Beth had connected at a deep level of trust. There was a lot more to their connection, but Drew could keep none of it if he couldn't keep her alive. And his adversary was a demon-driven man who, according to the Border Patrol, ranked high on the FBI's most wanted list.

Was Drew West up to this task? He knew some martial arts and quite a bit about guns. But the truth to that question frightened him.

Please, God. You've got to help me protect Beth.

"Drew, are you listening? I said here's what we'll do. When we get in town tomorrow, we go to the university, and I'll call them from my department's business phone."

"What department is that?"

"I have an MBA from Mays Business School."

"But I thought you were only—"

"Are you going to let me finish?"

He nodded.

"There won't be many people in the office now that summer school is going. And I can make sure no one is listening. I'll tell Sophia what's happening—no details—and I won't disclose your name. I'll give her a list of the things I'll need, have her box them up and drive to the Goodwill.

We'll get the box behind the building, and then we leave. But you need to stay out of sight the whole time. Then she won't know who I'm with or where I'm going. I'm just going out for several job interviews."

She was good. Drew put on a serious face. "You know, that's exactly what I was thinking."

Beth pursed her lips and socked him in the shoulder.

Drew grabbed a couch pillow and pounded her with it.

She grabbed the other pillow and swung round house at his head.

Drew ducked.

Beth missed, lost her balance, and fell against him. She ended up in his arms.

Before he could react, Beth kissed him.

As kisses go, it wasn't long. But it was long enough to release the emotions building up in him like a charge of electricity. When the voltage reached the necessary potential, it had jumped the gap between them.

The results, they peered into each other's eyes, breathing hard from their scuffle, both smiling after their discovery.

Drew cupped her cheek. "It's a good plan, Beth. Let's do it tomorrow."

"Yes, tomorrow. Because I don't think we should do that again tonight."

So Beth Sanchez was completely distracted after kissing him. "Agreed. I'll put it on tomorrow's agenda."

That earned him another punch in the shoulder.

Maybe she was only partly distracted.

She rubbed the spot on his shoulder in mock sympathy. "You can't schedule things like that. It would ruin them. Besides, we should get some sleep. It's a six-and-half hour drive to College Station. But I've got one more question for you."

"I thought only people like Suarez pounded other people to get information."

"That was just a love—a friendly little tap. I can hit a lot harder. Want to see?"

"I believe you. What did you want to ask me?"

She sat quietly for a moment studying him. "Where are you taking me, Drew West?"

At this point, he couldn't risk being too specific. Drew heaved a sigh. "My name should give you a clue."

"We're going west?"

"Yep. To a horse ranch."

Chapter 7

A loud buzz near Beth's head interrupted her dream. She opened her eyes and large red numbers screamed their message to her. 5:30 a.m. She turned off the annoying buzz.

Her horse was gone. Drew was gone. Well, the man in her dream seemed to be Drew. But then dreams never map directly to the reality of life. They are bent, skewed by the subconscious mind, or maybe they are, as Scrooge said after seeing Marley's ghost, a blot of mustard, a crumb of cheese eaten the evening before. But for Beth, the spicy Chick-fil-A sandwich was a more likely culprit.

A click and a thump came from the living room.

Drew must be up, turning his bed back into a couch.

Beth slid out of her bed and put on the last clean change of clothes she had in her pack.

A knock sounded on the bedroom door.

"Beth, are you up?"

She yawned. "I'm up."

"Are you decent?"

"Are you coming in?"

"That was my intent."

"Then I'm not decent." She grabbed her brush, ran it through her hair, and looked into the mirror.

This was as good as it would get this morning. She blew out a sigh. "I'm decent."

Drew stuck his head in. "Just got off the phone with Hunter. We need to leave ASAP."

"What's happening? Is everything—"

"Everything is fine. Were just taking some more precautions. Hunter rented us a car in his name, using his credit card. It's a one-way rental to Las Vegas. And I've got to get another cell phone before we leave town. So we need to go."

"Las Vegas? Do they have horse ranches there?"

"I don't know, but there will be a car waiting at the Las Vegas airport. Its owner is loaning the car to us. He lives near a horse ranch."

"In Nevada?"

"No. In Oregon."

"So I'm going to a horse ranch somewhere in Oregon?"

"To some of the most beautiful country in America."

If this had been a pleasure trip instead of fleeing to a hiding place, it would have been a dream vacation—riding horses in the American West. "Give me five minutes and I'll be ready to leave."

"Okay. I'll check us out of the room. Bring your things to the office when you're ready."

By 6:30 a.m., Drew had purchased a burner phone at Wal-Mart, and Beth was configuring it as Drew drove eastward on Interstate 10 in the Toyota minivan Hunter had rented and delivered to the Holiday Inn and Suites. The vehicle had tinted windows. That would make it difficult for anyone to recognize them as they drove by.

It seemed like a lot of trouble to cover their tracks, but with a clever, resourceful, and wealthy man like Hector Suarez, she and Drew had no choice. One misstep, one piece of information left in some business's database, or in cyberspace, could lead Suarez to them.

Drew and Beth had planned to get out of Texas and hide half a continent away. It was a good plan if they were meticulous in executing it. And Drew had accepted her input into the plan to get her things from Sophia's place in Bryan. He had treated her like an equal, not like some fragile female who might be bruised by a pea twenty mattresses underneath her. And he respected her strength, as proven when he smacked her on the head with the pillow last night. All things considered, this arrangement appeared to be working out far better than Beth had hoped. The horse ranch was frosting on the cake.

As a result, Beth had, for the first time since her father's death, opened her heart enough to let another male inside the door.

Girl, you did more than let him inside the door. You kissed him.

"It wasn't actually a kiss, not a real one." She had done it again. Having a conversation with oneself is fine if a person were alone. And Beth spent a lot of time alone. But this time—

"It seemed real to me."

"That's not what I meant."

"Yeah. So you say now. It wasn't real at all. How did it feel, Beth? Real or phony?"

"Drew ... sometimes I talk to myself. Okay? You'll just have to get used to it. Don't pay any attention when I do that. It's mostly nonsense."

"I agree."

"If you'll stop bothering me, I'll finish setting up your new cell phone. And don't you have something better to do like making sure no one is following us?"

"Nobody is following us ... except that sixteen-wheeler that keeps bugging me. Doesn't he have cruise control?" Drew glanced her way. "Beth, how's your ankle?"

"The swelling is much better. It's fine, unless I try to run on it."

"That's good. But we should pick up some adhesive tape first time we get a chance."

Was Drew worried or just being cautious? "Tape's not very comfortable. Do you think I need to be ready to run at a moment's notice?"

"I hope not. But when we get to Oregon, we'll be riding horses."

The smile on her face grew "Real horses? Not ponies or plow horses?"

"Yep. Quarter horses. Equine dragsters. Can you ride?"

"My ancestors were Spaniards. Horses are in my genes."

"I'd say it's more like Spanish royalty in your jeans. I mean your jean shorts."

"It's shocking what goes through men's minds."

"Using my words against me? I can see I'll have to watch what I say."

"No. Just don't say what you watch." She gave him her best imitation of a smirky smile.

"Fine. I'll watch in silence ... are you really a blue-blooded Spaniard?"

"Only the part of me that's not Native American."

"You've got Native Americans in Mexico?"

"Sure. Yaquis, Aztecs, Mayans, Apaches, Zapotecs, several tribes, just to name a few."

"Which are you?"

"Aztec ... we think. What are you, Drew?"

"I'm a mutt."

"Come on. If I have to tell, so do you."

"Okay. German, English, and enough Cherokee to be a member of the tribe."

"So we're both European mixed with indigenous tribes."

"Yeah. But I have a strong suspicion that you are a lot more blue-blooded than you're admitting."

She didn't like discussing her aristocratic Spanish history. Beth Sanchez was from a middle-class family, nothing special. "Drew, we have people trying to find us and kill us. You don't seem to be worried about that."

"I'm not worried, yet. The first real shot at us—if Suarez has the resources you described—"

"He has a lot of resources. Don't underestimate him."

Drew's eyes took on the intense look she had seen when Drew confronted Suarez by the river. "That won't happen, Beth. His first chance of finding us comes when we get to College Station and you contact your relatives."

Drew was right. Beth needed to weigh every word when she talked to Sophia. Saying the wrong thing could get Sophia, Beth, and Drew killed.

* * *

Suarez's phone rang and played the Hawaii Five-0 theme. He looked at the display. 1:15 p.m. It was a call from Ramon. Maybe it was good news.

"*El Capitan*, here."

"Hector, she just called her aunt or cousin, whoever lives here."

"But you do not have the capability to listen to the call, so what did you find out?"

"She called from a number at the University. Probably to set up a rendezvous. The girl will want some of her things if she's not coming back to stay."

"That is correct. Watch the house, Ramon. If anyone leaves, follow them."

"If I spot West and Sanchez, what should I do?"

"You don't have the kind of weapons to ensure they will be killed. Get the vehicle description and license plate number. Once I have that information, we can make plans to upstage this grand event being planned in Pecos. Having no witnesses means no case and no trial. Call me as soon as you have seen them."

Suarez ended the call and placed another call to a former Special Forces soldier, a weapons sergeant, now a meth head. His brains weren't completely fried, yet. He could give Hector a whole smorgasbord of weapons to choose from to blow up a car. And the sergeant had most of them in his weapons cache.

Now, Suarez just needed to know which vehicle to obliterate.

* * *

Beth turned in at the strip mall entrance and drove the van behind a large Goodwill store.

Drew had curled up in the passenger-side floorboard. It was best that Sophia not see him or hear his name.

Beth parked the van so she wouldn't block the unloading area at the rear of the store. The trees and adjacent buildings blocked the view behind the Goodwill store for anyone not in back of the building.

There was no one there. Only Drew and Beth.

After a minute or two, Sophia's minivan rounded the corner.

Beth stuck her arm out the window and waved at Sophia, then pushed the button to open the rear door of the van.

Sophia pulled alongside, stopped, and transferred two cardboard boxes to the back of Beth's van, then she turned to walk to the driver's window.

Beth gave her the palms-out stop signal. "Sophia, I'm going to be gone on some job interviews for a while. You may read things about me in the newspaper, or see something on TV about a certain drug lord—"

"No! No! Beth, you must not follow in your father's—"

"I'm not. I'm just an accidental witness to something. But for you, all you know is that I left for job interviews."

"Your life is in danger, is it not? Shouldn't you be under US Marshal's protection?"

"I've got the best protection I can possibly have. Now go before anyone sees us together. Don't go straight home though. Run an errand or go to the grocery store. Okay?"

Sophia nodded and turned away, then turned back toward Beth. "I will be praying for you, Beth. May God be with you."

"Yes. Please pray for us—uh, for me."

Sophia's eyebrows raised. She nodded and then left.

Beth powered her window up and relaxed, hidden again behind the tinted glass.

"Beth," Drew's strained voice sounded as uncomfortable as he looked. "Give her two minutes, then we'll leave. We can't let anyone know we rendezvoused here."

"No one could've seen us, unless they were already in the building or at the loading dock."

"Good. Now, if I can just get out of the floorboard before my back muscles start spasming." Drew crawled up onto the seat, turned around, and sat. "Sixty seconds more, then we get out of Dodge."

"But we're in a Toyota."

"Yeah. Not quite a sneeze mobile."

"A what?"

"It's not a Subaru, Isuzu, or a Mitsubishi. You're not from around here, are you?" He grinned.

"You and your American friends have corrupted the King's English, Drew West."

"You and your friends have corrupted the drug lords."

Somehow the puns and jokes had degenerated into sharp barbs that jabbed the wounds on Beth's heart. Drew might not realize how much his words hurt. But she couldn't ignore the fact that they had, because Drew had joked about the very things her father gave his life trying to change.

It was quiet in the van for the next hour.

* * *

Suarez hadn't heard from Ramon in three hours. It was too long. There must be bad news.

He hit Ramon's entry in his contacts.

After five rings, Hector was ready to end the call, but Ramon answered.

"This is Ramon."

"Did you locate them?"

"I'm working on that."

"That is no answer, Ramon. You missed them, didn't you?"

"Let me call you back in five minutes. Perhaps I will have good news."

"Five minutes, Ramon." Suarez ended the call. "Or I may have some very bad news for you."

Ramon had five seconds left of his five-minute limit when Hector's phone rang.

"*El Capitan*, here."

"Hector, I think we have the license plate and the vehicle description."

"What happened, Ramon? How did they lose you?"

"Let me explain. Ms. Sanchez's cousin made two stops after leaving her house. One was at a Goodwill store where she met Elizabeth Sanchez behind the store. I posed as an undercover policeman and asked the store manager to see the security video. I now have a positive ID on Ms. Sanchez. We saw her through the open window of the van. Mr. West was probably in the van with her. The windows were dark. We could not see inside. They are driving a black Toyota Sienna minivan with Texas license plate DBX-0998. It is a rented van, so we do not know how long they will have it."

It was useful information. But only useful in keeping Ramon on the job. Maybe that was Ramon's idea. There wasn't much Suarez could do about that except ... keep Ramon on the job. "Find out which company the van belongs to and make sure you will be notified the minute it is turned in. I'm sure some employee of the car rental company thinks it's worth it to notify you if you paid them say … $50,000 for the information. Money is no object. Find them, Ramon!"

Chapter 8

"I've been thinking, Beth."

"Maybe I should be worried." She gave Drew her best attempt at a smirk.

"Seriously, what do you think would be the easiest way for Suarez to learn that we're in this rental van?"

The tingling between her shoulder blades sent shivers through Beth's upper body.

"I'm stopping right now and you're driving." She pulled off from Highway 6 onto a side road.

Drew powered his window down part way and looked at the road sign beside them. "Old Marlin Road?"

"Yes. The place where Drew West starts driving."

"Beth, what's gotten into you?"

"The easiest way for Suarez to spot us is if I'm driving and he spots me."

"Texas is a big state. What are the odds that one of his stooges is standing at—uh, Old Marlin Road, outside of Waco, Texas, looking for Beth Sanchez to drive by?"

"Bigger than you might think."

"What's going on?"

She blew out a sharp sigh. "When you asked that question, I just got this creepy feeling that I shouldn't be driving."

"That I can understand. But to think Suarez might be standing here and—"

"Señor?" A man with swarthy skin rapped on Drew's window. He had black hair and a Spanish accent.

"Go, Beth!"

She hit the accelerator and the van sprayed the man with gravel until the Sienna fishtailed out onto Highway 6.

Beth glanced at Drew. "See what I mean?"

"It was just a harmless old man. Probably wanted directions."

"Hence 'go, Beth'?" She glanced his way.

Drew didn't reply.

If Suarez found them, that's not how it would happen, but it still freaked her out as much as that Hispanic man had Drew. "You know, the most likely way Suarez would find us is to bribe a few car rental agents to search their database until he found your rental record for this van. Then he would know the van's description, license plate number, and where and when you planned to turn it in. He could be waiting for us in Las Vegas."

"You're right, but it won't be quite as easy as you described. Hunter rented the van."

"Did he list you as an authorized driver? If he didn't, I hope the police don't stop us. They might think we stole the van."

"I don't know and it doesn't really matter. You worry too much. But I can still drive if you want me to."

"Please, will you, Drew?"

Drew fiddled with the GPS for a few seconds. "We'll cross Lake Waco in a couple of miles. Take the first exit beyond the lake. There's a gas station. We can fill up and, while I drive, you can find a place for us to spend the night."

"Okay. I'll look for a place in Clovis."

"New Mexico?"

"Barely in New Mexico. Like you said, Texas is a big state. It takes all day to drive across it."

"Basically, we'll have done it twice since six o'clock this morning. Fort Stockton to College Station and back."

"But not back to Fort Stockton. That's almost three hundred miles south of Clovis and a lot farther from Oregon."

"Since you know the state so well, maybe you should keep driving."

"No. I can just tell you where to go, Drew."

"I'll bet you can. Your eyes have done that a couple of times since we met. Like when I was checking you out after you sprained your ankle."

"That's because you didn't stop with my ankle."

"What does this have to do with evading Suarez?"

"Nothing ... everything—I don't know."

"Beth ... you're afraid you're leading Suarez to Oregon, aren't you?"

"Here's the exit. You're driving now."

"Not talking about it doesn't make it go away."

She exited and slowed to turn in at the gas station.

"This is about you feeling guilty for—"

"Can we talk about something else?" She'd never told him she felt guilty, only that her family was killed.

"You are smart, educated, beautiful, and you're a good woman. You're not defective or guilty or ..." He shook his head. "The only thing that surprises me is that some guy hasn't already snatched you up."

"Nobody can just snatch me up, Drew West." She shot him a glaring glance.

"Then can I be nobody?"

"That's who's going to be riding with me if someone doesn't respect my boundaries." Drew never stopped pushing. Was it going to be like this for two thousand miles? She pulled up to the gas pump and stopped.

Drew grabbed the door handle. "Nobody, huh? I'll gas up the car if you promise not to drive away without me."

"With me, you just have to take your chances."

"I have been, and I think it's worked out pretty well, don't you?"

"Do you know how to pump gas, or am I going to have to do it?" Drew couldn't be that clueless. If she wasn't ready to talk about something, he needed to respect her wishes.

"I'm just going to say this one time and then I'll shut up."

"Good. Then we can have two thousand miles of peace."

Drew's sigh blasted from his mouth. "Even if Suarez were to follow us to Oregon, it wouldn't be your fault. It was my idea and it was a good one, considering our circumstances. If he finds us, I'm to blame and I'll deal with it."

"Are you finished?"

"Yeah. Completely." Drew shoved the door open and closed it harder than necessary. Then he couldn't find the gas tank.

Beth could see it from the driver's sideview mirror. She powered down her window. "It's on this side, Drew. Deal with it."

He strode around the van, opened the gas tank, jammed the nozzle down its throat, gritted his teeth, and clamped hard on the handle.

Beth had never seen a tank filled that quickly.

So Drew had a temper too. But he was usually right on target when he analyzed her. Maybe she should apologize. But only if he would drop the subject of her guilt feelings about Suarez and the Laguna massacre.

She opened her door, circled around the front of the car and got in on the passenger's side.

Drew closed the tank and climbed into the driver's seat.

When his right hand reached for the ignition, she laid her hand on his arm. "I'm sorry, Drew. Really."

He nodded, started the car, and pulled onto the street.

Was he going to be stubborn about his remark, *just going to say this one time*? That would be childish. And he had to know she didn't want silence all the way to Oregon. Beth studied his face as he stared down the road.

After Drew merged with the traffic on the highway, he glanced at her. "Just so you know, nobody's in the car with you and he's snatching you up, Beth Sanchez." He gave her the silly grin that you see on a kid's face when they chant that children's taunting jingle.

Drew studied her eyes for a second or two. "Na nana nana na."

Beth couldn't hold in her laugh. It came out in a belly-shaking burst that worked wonders for her mood. But how had Drew known what she was thinking? For the third or fourth time, his ability to read her seemed uncanny, like one-way mental telepathy.

"Drew?" She put her hand on his arm.

"Yeah." He glanced her way.

"If you'll do that one more time, I'll consider ..."

"Consider letting me snatch you up. It's a deal. Na nana nana na."

That wasn't what she had in mind, but Beth didn't correct him. With the uncertain future they faced, they could both use a little fantasy.

Over five-hundred miles and eight hours after leaving College Station, Drew pulled into the Clovis Inn and Suites, a place Beth had found using his cell. Suites were only sixty-eight dollars a night. That seemed like a bargain.

After checking in, they carried their packs to the room. Drew unlocked the door and pushed it open.

Beth could see why the rate was cheap. "This isn't going to work, Drew."

A wall down the center of their suite divided the room into two halves. One half was the living room, the other a bedroom with two queen beds.

"We can make it work. I'll sleep on the couch."

After a fast-food dinner from a place across the street, Beth crawled into one of the queen-size beds. Fatigue claimed her body in seconds then, in a couple of minutes, took her consciousness too.

Familiar images scrolled across her field of vision. Smoke and the nauseating odor of death choked her. Flames still licked at the remains of her house, as they did at buildings throughout the town of Laguna.

No policemen. No authorities of any kind. No people. They were either dead or had fled the violence. Out of the flames a figure approached her. A second figure followed. Rafael Sanchez, her father, reached out a hand and beckoned Beth to follow.

Beth gasped and sat up in her bed. Her eyes darted around the unfamiliar room looking for anything to remove the images from her mind.

"Beth?" A tall, shadowy form appeared at the far end of the wall. "You yelled something. Are you okay?"

"No." She wasn't okay. She would never be okay. And she couldn't help but reach out for Drew.

She stood and he wrapped her up in his arms.

"Hey. Whatever it was, was only a dream. Dreams aren't reality, but they can sure seem like it. You're safe, Beth, and I intend to keep you that way."

He released her and led her around the wall into the living room.

They sat on the couch.

"Do you want to talk about it, or talk about something else?"

Drew would discover it all sooner or later. The way he read her, probably sooner. And he needed to know about her strengths, her weaknesses, especially her fears. It could be important if they were in danger.

"I have dreams sometimes. The dreams stopped two years ago, about the time I started graduate school. But after the incident with Suarez at the river, they're back."

"How do they make you feel?"

"They frighten me. Make me relive horrifying events and memories. Then each dream ends with Papa, uh, my father, motioning for me to follow him and Mama. To join them in death. It's what I deserve." Tears came. She couldn't stop them.

Drew pulled her head against his chest and held her while she cried. No words this time. No pushing or forcing anything. He simply stroked her head and held her until she cried her fear and pain away.

After a few minutes, Beth sat up and swiped at her wet cheeks. "I need a tissue."

He went into the bathroom and returned with a handful.

She wiped her eyes, blew her nose, and then looked up at Drew.

It was kind of him to start with asking about her feelings. But eventually, he needed to hear the whole story. Not just suspect that she felt guilty, but to know why she *was* guilty. He needed to know what she had done.

"You heard part of the story from that Border Patrol guy, Coy. But there's more to it."

"Yeah. I figured there was."

"You heard about the Laguna massacre. What Suarez did. But no description can capture the awfulness of it. The sickening odor of burned bodies and ..." She needed to get on to the issues. Not dwell on the horror.

"About my father, Rafael Sanchez ... you need to know that I admired him, loved him, and he loved me. Called me his *precioso tesoro*, precious treasure. But after Suarez retaliated for my father's militia driving the cartel out of the region, I was torn between admiring him and thinking of him as a fool."

"I can understand that. But if you fight for what's right, Beth, you're never a fool. Maybe he could have been wiser, but a good heart doesn't make any man a fool. But then my thoughts are not the issue. And I'm thinking this isn't really the source of your guilt. Right?"

"I don't know how you do that, Drew. And I don't know whether to be afraid of you seeing everything about me or to be glad that you do."

"We're getting off track here. But, Beth, I will never use what I learn about you to hurt you. Never. If that ever happens, it's not my intent. So, if you want to tell me more ..."

Maybe not tomorrow or even later tonight, but right now, she trusted Drew. And she needed to tell him before she closed all the windows and locked all the doors to that place of shame and guilt that resided where the real Beth Sanchez lived and existed.

"The day before the attack, my two best friends, Maria and Alejandra, asked me to go to a young people's dance club about thirty miles away in another town. It wasn't a bad place, but it wasn't one my parents approved of. They had forbidden me to go there. But I snuck away after dinner that evening. Told my parents I was spending the night with Maria, but we went to the club and stayed there until nearly one o'clock in the morning. We only had fun. We didn't do anything wrong, except that I had lied to my mother and my father. I should have been at home. I should have been killed with them. But I lied and I'm alive. I have to live with that every day."

"So you believe you should be dead?"

"If I were a good daughter, I would be dead."

"None of us are perfect. And didn't God tell us he numbered the hairs on our head. He didn't count them. He numbered them … just like he did with the days of our lives. For those of us who trust Him, we leave our life in His hands. I can't explain the sovereignty of God to you. I can't understand it myself. I'm finite and He is infinite. The finite me can only understand that part of the infinite God that He explains to me. But I believe He is sovereign over our lives. That means He has reasons for Beth Sanchez being alive. There's a purpose behind it. And I'm glad He wants you alive, or I would never have known you. Who knows, maybe there's a purpose in that too."

Drew hadn't told her anything she didn't already know. He had simply reminded her of things she needed to hear. And, in doing that, he had done it again. It seemed he had read her heart and spoken directly to its need.

The dark cloud that came with her dream had fled. It dumped its rain and evaporated into the atmosphere.

She leaned close to Drew and kissed his cheek. "Thanks."

Beth had expected to see that winning smile on his face, but she got the intense look that said Drew West was serious about something.

His eyes softened. "Marry me, Beth. I have a contract for what will be my breakout novel. There are speaking engagements, writing conferences, courses to teach. I need a business manager, someone who can take all the opportunities and turn them into profit. I can't do all that and write."

"Not even forty-eight hours and you're proposing to me? You really do storm the castle. Hunter warned me about you."

"Hunter is Mr. hyperbole. Nothing is as bad or as good as he says. Just like his Big Bend excursions business. It didn't fold. There was a downturn for maybe a day, and now it's booming again. Hunter even has stories to tell about catching cartel mules. He's benefited from all that, just like I have. No. Nothing like what I found in you, Beth."

She tried to interrupt him, but Drew continued. "My life was on a long detour to places I didn't want to go until this beautiful señorita tried to give me the cold shoulder and ended up giving me her sprained ankle. Do you want me to tell you what I was thinking as I held your ankle and checked it out?"

"You don't really admit to thinking stuff like that, do you?"

"Thanks for the vote of confidence. On what basis are you accusing me of inappropriate thoughts? Your own experience?"

"Okay. What were you thinking about when you were holding my sexy, swollen ankle?"

"That I wanted to take care of you for the rest of my life."

"Drew, real life isn't like a Charles Martin or Nicholas Sparks romance. You don't love someone a few hours after meeting them."

"Maybe not. But it's easy to imagine it, after you meet the right person."

"Okay. Imagine it. But give us some time. After my INTJ personality grates on you for a while, you'll probably have some reservations about me. People like me aren't affectionate. We can be quite annoying, and we aren't very lovable."

"Your words might say that. But your eyes make up for it. They betray the real Beth Sanchez."

"And what are those eyes saying right now?"

"That you wanted to say yes but didn't want anyone thinking you were a fool. So you will say yes, but only after you give us a little more time."

She sensed a major frown wrinkling her forehead.

"It's okay. I can wait until tomorrow." Drew grinned.

She punched him in the shoulder, but there was no strength in her arm. Her strength had drained away with the realization that she had no place to hide anything from Drew West, not even in the frontal lobes of her brain.

That was disconcerting. But it was more than disconcerting to realize that Drew could read Beth better than she could read herself.

Tonight's proposal had been an attempt to feel her out before the real thing. But when Drew read her heart and then pushed the issue, could he, as he said, just snatch her up?

I don't have to answer that ... yet.

Chapter 9

Hector Suarez ended his call to Luis Santana, head of the revived Tijuana Cartel, and he revisited each point of the agreement he had just made with his peer on the West Coast.

The agreement would be a mutually beneficial one, a treaty of sorts. And it opened new vistas for forward-thinking cartel leaders. And for taking advantage of those who were mentally inferior to Hector Suarez.

If he had to chase Drew West and Elizabeth Sanchez to a West Coast location, such as Oregon, Hector would be intruding on the sales area of the Tijuana Cartel. And he did not need a confrontation with them when the Del Rio organization already had to fend off attacks and intrusions by Los Zetas, a common enemy of the Del Rio and Tijuana cartels.

Hector had promised to aid the Tijuana organization by distracting the Zetas, using a variety of threats whenever the Zetas encroached on Tijuana territory either in Mexico or on their sales regions in the US. In return, Luis Santana would assist Hector when he made his move against the arrogant little—he swore each time the thought of Mr. West. And that happened every time Hector's knee throbbed. About once a minute.

A stabbing pain shot through his sore knee. He tried to adjust the knee brace through his Armani slacks. Hector swore again when the brace refused to yield to his fingers through the fabric.

As he struggled with the brace, his cell rang. The theme from Hawaii Five-0, Ramon's ringtone.

Throbbing knee or not, Hector needed to talk to him.

"Ramon, here. I think I have some good news."

"You *think* so? Then I *think* I will wait until I hear what you have before I get excited."

"Hector, you are too much a pessimist."

"You mean a realist?"

"Let me make you an optimist. I have found where Drew West's family lives in Oregon."

"And why should he return there? I hear it rains all the time in Oregon."

"Not where Drew's family has their horse ranch. It is on the east side of the Cascade Mountains."

"That is what—fifteen-hundred miles from Texas?"

"Maybe a little more. But it is a remote area near Redmond, along the Deschutes River. It is an area of many rivers, mountains, canyons—badlands for a bad boy to hide with his señorita."

"Maybe Mr. West goes to Oregon and maybe not. But he will go, as his name says, west. People choose places they know well when they want to hide."

"*Si, El Capitan.* So I should go west too."

El Capitan? Ramon is buttering me up to ask a favor.

"Yes, you should go west."

"Good. Then I will go to Las Vegas to wait for word that the rental car is returned. From there, I can quickly reach any of the western states. Many flights each day come into Las Vegas. And, perhaps, I can have a little fun while I am waiting."

"On your own time, Ramon. Not on mine. Very well. Go to Las Vegas."

"Once we find them, do you need me to—"

"No. Your job is only to find them. It is not your concern how I take them or how I dispense with them. If I need you for anything else related to West and Sanchez, I will tell you."

He ended the call.

"And if you botch this job, Ramon, I will dispense with you as painfully as I will with Mr. West and the Señorita.

Chapter 10

Drew handed the rental contract to the attendant at the McCarran Rent-A-Car Center just south of the airport in Las Vegas.

The thirty-something Hispanic man scanned the papers then jerked as if he'd been slapped. "One moment, sir. I've got to take this call."

Drew watched the man's fingers key in a number before he turned away and muffled his voice.

"Beth, he said *take* a call not *make* a call."

"Drew, let's get out of here as fast as we can. Something doesn't feel right."

"Yeah. I've never liked those zingers running up the back of my neck either."

After a short phone conversation, the attendant turned back toward them. "May I ask you to wait a moment, sir, while we check the car for—"

"There are no damages and you've got my credit card. Just tell me how to get to the Terminal One parking garage. We're running late."

"But it will only take a moment, and it will speed things up if you—"

"I don't have a moment and *you* need to speed things up."

The man's eyes widened. "Yes, sir. You can wait in the lobby for the shuttle. I can tell you when it arrives."

"When it arrives? Isn't that the shuttle stopping out front?"

"Oh. It's already here. This shuttle will take you to Terminal One. It stops at the front of the terminal. Just walk through the terminal building to the other side and you'll see the parking garage straight ahead."

"Come on, Beth. Let's go."

As they strode to the shuttle, Beth took his arm. "He just called Suarez."

"He wanted us to miss the next shuttle. He probably called one of Suarez's thugs, or someone Suarez paid off, to let them know when we arrived. But they don't know what we plan to do here. So when we get off that shuttle, Beth, we need to get lost in the crowd as fast as we can. We can't afford for anyone to recognize us getting into that vehicle Mom's rancher friend left for us."

* * *

Ramon's cell buzzed his leg from where he'd put it in his pants pocket. He glanced at the display. Roundabout Car Rentals. He didn't know whether to curse or celebrate. If this was about Señor West and Señorita Sanchez, he had done his job, but it also meant his Vegas vacation was over.

"This is Ramon Vazquez."

"Sir, you asked me to call if they showed up. They just turned in their car."

Ramon strode toward the entrance to Harrah's Hotel and Casino. "Can you stall them. I'm on my way to the airport."

"I will try, sir."

Ramon ended the call. At the street, he flagged down a taxi. "One-hundred bucks if you can get me to the airport car rental center in five minutes."

After he slid in, a college-age man with a short beard turned to get a better look at Ramon. "It's five and a half miles to the rental car center. How much is it worth if I simply try my best?"

It was not going to get any better than that. "Okay. A hundred bucks if you will do anything short of wrecking us to get me there."

"You got it."

Ramon hit Suarez's speed dial number.

"What's happening, Ramon?"

"*Puedes creerlo?* Señor West and the Señorita are turning in their rental car at the *Las Vegas Airport*, and I am only four minutes away in a cab."

"We are most fortunate to have picked Las Vegas. If they have left the rental center, pay the man to tell you where they went. If you find them now, Ramon, they are ours. Do not fail me." Suarez ended the call.

Ramon grabbed the handle above the door and hung on as the cab driver picked his way through traffic at an incredible rate.

The quick maneuvers slammed Ramon against the window and then slid his rear half-way across the seat. He held onto the handle in what seemed like a fight for his life.

He covered his eyes with his free hand as they blasted through a large intersection. The light had been red when they entered but must have turned green as they sailed by the crosswalk. The driver's uncanny sense of the timing of the light changes had bought Ramon some time.

Six minutes later, the cab screeched to a stop in front of the rental center.

Ramon tossed the cabbie a hundred-dollar bill and then scanned the windows until he saw the logo for Roundabout Rentals.

Before he could reach the counter, a man wearing a Roundabout shirt walked toward him. "Mr. Vazquez?"

"Yes." Ramon handed the man a hundred-dollar bill. "Which way did they go?"

"The man and the hot chick?"

"Yes. Them."

"If I tell you, will something bad happen to them?"

"No. I am only a private investigator who needs to find them and ask them some questions ... for my client."

The young man looked at the bill, then back at Ramon. "They caught the shuttle to Terminal One. That's it making the turn onto the street."

"Did they say where they were going? Anything might help me?"

"They asked for directions to the parking garage for that terminal."

Ramon turned to tell the cab driver to wait.

The cab sped away to the street.

He turned back to the agent. "When does the next shuttle come?"

The agent pointed out the window toward the freeway. "See it turning onto Gillespie?"

"And where do I find the man and the, as you say it, hot chick at the terminal?"

"They will go through the terminal to the other side. You'll see the signs to the parking garage. It's straight ahead."

So someone had provided them a car. They would pick up a privately owned car and disappear into the Vegas traffic.

Ramon would be about five minutes behind them.

How long would it take someone to find a car, put their things in, check out the controls, and drive away?

About five minutes.

He strode out to meet the incoming shuttle.

It poked along the semi-circle driveway at an infuriating pace.

Darse prisa, tonto!

* * *

Drew and Beth had lost a couple of minutes getting lost in the crowd inside the terminal. It was now 9:00 p.m. The sun had been down for almost an hour, and it would soon be dark. That might help hide them as they left.

Drew spotted the vehicle in the space Hunter had mentioned. It was an older model Dodge pickup with a king cab.

Drew took Beth's bag from her and tossed both of their bags in the back seat.

Beth laid her hand on his shoulder. "Uh, Drew ... "

"What, Beth? We need to go."

"My clothes ... the stuff Sophia packed for me. It's all in the back of the—"

"Sorry. But we can't go back. I'll take you shopping in Redmond and buy you a whole new wardrobe if you'll just get in this truck so we can get out of Dodge."

"Don't you mean get into the Dodge?"

"We don't have time for English lessons."

"Was that an insult?"

Rapid footsteps echoed through the garage.

"Doesn't matter. Just get in. There's someone running through the parking garage, and I don't want to wait to see who it is."

Beth pulled Drew down between the truck and an SUV parked beside it.

The dim parking-garage lights revealed an Hispanic man sprinting toward them with a cell phone held to his ear.

The runner stopped a couple of vehicles away and scanned the area around him.

The tingling running up the back of Drew's neck turned to a higher voltage, maybe two-twenty. He placed his mouth beside Beth's ear. "We need to get out of here, now."

The truck had been backed in. Beth circled behind it, near the wall, and now stood at the passenger-side door.

They opened their doors in synch. The interior lights lit them up like mid-day as they climbed in.

Drew grabbed the truck keys under the dash, where Hunter said they would be, and stuck them in the ignition. "He's bound to have seen us."

"You got that right. He's walking our way."

"We need to make a run for it. Unless ... Beth, I could beat the tar out of the guy, tie him up, and force him to go with us, then dump him out in the desert."

"What if he has a gun?"

"Right." Drew pulled out of the parking space, with the rear wheels burning rubber, and he headed straight at the man.

He dove out of the way, landing on the concrete in front of a sports car.

In the rear-view mirror, before the man disappeared from sight, he held his cell with both hands and pointed it at them.

* * *

"It was them, Suarez."

"Did you get the vehicle description and license plate number?"

"It was an old pickup. Maybe a Dodge. It had Oregon plates. I shot a picture with my cell, but I cannot read the license number. It was too dark."

"*No importa.* It is obvious where they are going, Ramon. They go to Mr. West's family's home. I need you to go there and watch them until I arrive."

"So you are coming, Hector?"

"I have been waiting for this for almost eight years. Yes, I am coming, and I will bring a force so powerful it will wipe all traces of Señor West and Señorita Sanchez off the face of the earth. It will be like they never lived."

And soon they won't.

Chapter 11

"He got our picture with his cell. What are we going to do?" Beth stared at Drew obviously waiting for a reply.

Drew had always created a course of action with each change in their precarious situation. But only one thing came to mind. It was the curse of being a writer.

Use a dodge to get out of Dodge in the Dodge.

He started to share his clever pun, but the scowl on Beth's face said it wouldn't be a good idea. Instead, he studied the traffic ahead and then accelerated down the expressway to the left-turn lane.

The light was green, so Drew didn't slow much as he took the sharp turn from 593 to 515 North.

The tires on the big Dodge pickup squealed their complaint.

He merged into the light traffic on 515. "I didn't see anyone following us. But we need to make sure we've lost Suarez's stooge. He's probably figured out we're going to Oregon. These plates are a dead giveaway."

"Drew ... you could have made a better word choice." Her almond-shaped, brown eyes studied him, though it was too dark to read them.

"Even if he does know we're headed for Oregon, we don't want him ambushing us on the way, especially when we stop tonight."

"Is it safe for us to stop? Maybe we should keep driving."

"Beth, after two long days and a short night, it's probably not safe for *me* to keep driving." Drew paused. "Here's what we'll do. We're gonna go west on US 95. See if you can find an out-of-the-way place to stop for the night, some place about three hours down the road."

He glanced at the clock on the dash. "It's a little after nine o'clock. If we can stop by midnight, the offices of most motels should be open."

"What if we're followed?"

"Out in the desert at night, we'll be able to spot anyone following us. If we see a suspicious vehicle, I'll lose it."

Beth played with Drew's cell for about five minutes, then looked up at him. If you can keep up this pace, there's a Best Western at Tonopah, about three hours away. It says they have suites but, like last night, the pictures show one bedroom and a living room with a couch."

"That works. I can sleep on the couch. But hopefully, it won't be like last night."

"You mean my nightmare?" Beth lowered her voice to a whisper. "When you held me, no nightmares. I slept just fine."

"That's not a good idea. We've already thrown caution to the wind because of our circumstances. But holding a beautiful woman like Beth Sanchez all night ..."

"Forget I mentioned it."

"I can't, now that you mentioned it. It's all I can think about." He grinned at her.

"I never know when you're teasing or serious. Or are you trying to lure me into dropping my guard?"

"Beth, you dropped it about twenty-four hours ago. Now you're dealing with the consequences ... me."

She didn't reply.

"You know, tomorrow we still have a ten-hour drive to get to the ranch."

"This has been a long, tiring drive, and we still have six hundred miles to go?" Beth yawned.

"Blame it on Texas. It took an entire day just to get out of the state." Drew checked the road behind them.

Beth had watched him peering into the rearview mirror. "Is anyone following us?"

"We're out in the desert, and there aren't any cars in view behind us. We're safe, for now."

Beth laid her head against the seat with her face turned toward him. She propped a hand on his shoulder.

For the next two hours, she appeared to cat nap. With all that had happened, the stress and short nights, she was probably running on fumes.

Maybe it was Drew's wishful thinking but, in the darkness of the pickup cab, it looked like she smiled from time to time.

Her hand had slid off his shoulder and onto the seat.

Drew took it and squeezed. "Hey, we're almost to that Best Western in Tonopah."

After Drew checked them in, they both carried their packs into the room.

He dropped his on the floor.

Beth put hers on the couch and unzipped it. "Drew, we need to stop somewhere tomorrow morning. I'm meeting your mother tomorrow, and I don't have any clean clothes. Except what we left in those two boxes in the van."

"We can stop somewhere and get you some clothes."

She went into the bathroom and came out wearing the shorts and t-shirt she'd slept in last night. But instead of going into the bedroom, she hung around the couch and fiddled with her pack.

"I thought you'd be asleep by now. Did you sleep too much on the way here?"

Beth shook her head. "Last night you learned all about me, all the fear and the ugliness in my past. But I need to know more about Drew West, especially since he thinks I'm about to say yes to his marriage proposal."

"About that ... I was only joking ... well, joking a little bit ... and maybe hinting and hoping."

"Regardless, I still need to know why you are the way you are."

"What's that supposed to mean?"

"You always seem to be spoiling for a fight. You have a short fuse, and it seems like you have a big chip on your shoulder."

"Beth, I've never acted that way toward you."

"I know you haven't. And you don't toward Hunter either. But for people you don't know as well, you get angry so fast that you could get yourself in trouble. You know, like you almost did with that US Attorney, Whittaker. Would you care to explain how you got that chip on your shoulder?"

"You said it, Beth. I have a short temper."

"Why? I know something is driving you when you get that way. And when you're protecting something or someone—"

"You mean someone like you?"

"Yes. I told you the truth about me. I need the same from Drew West or this relationship is going nowhere."

"So we *do* have a relationship?"

"Drew ... I kissed you. I've never done that with a guy before ... ever. Now quit jockeying for position, or evading, and explain Drew West to me. Tell me why you have this over-the-top desire to protect and serve and why you do it so fiercely."

Drew sighed and sat on the couch. He patted a spot beside him.

Beth sat, but she slid against him and laid her head on his shoulder. She was near, but he didn't have to look into her eyes.

INTJ girl was doing what she always seemed be doing, thinking and calculating. That meant she had purposely created this intimate, non-threatening environment to make it easier for him to talk to her. Beth was nurturing a relationship with him in INTJ fashion.

Based on what he'd observed over the past two and a half days, this was a major breakthrough. If he wanted a permanent relationship with this woman, he needed to tell her his story.

Drew searched for an opening to his story, but couldn't find a good spot to jump in.

Beth took his hand. "When that Border Patrol agent insinuated that I was Ricardo's girlfriend, you said I was *yours*." Beth spoke softly, and for the first time, he heard a hint of a Spanish accent. "It wasn't so much what you said, but the way you said it. 'No. She's mine.' So fierce that I thought you might attack him. When Whittaker insinuated you couldn't keep me safe, you nearly assaulted him. I thought he might arrest you. He seems the type to abuse his authority. Why, Drew?"

Beth had given him the starting point for his story, one that met her specifications. He needed to go with it.

"About seventeen years ago, when I was ten, my grandfather gave me my first rifle. It was a Christmas gift. A .22 lever-action rifle. It wasn't new, but it was a nice gun. I thought I was grown up. I'd passed to manhood in the West family."

"Is that unusually young for getting a gun?"

"Not where we lived. One guy I knew got a .22 when he was seven. But it's what you do or don't do with a gun that shows you're grown up."

"What did you do with your gun at ten years of age?"

"Mostly I went plinking in the woods. But it was what I didn't do that was the problem." He paused. "A couple of months after I got my gun, a burglar broke into our house during the night. I woke up first, heard some strange sounds, so I got my gun and stepped out of my room. Down the hallway, a man dressed in dark clothing stood like he was trying to decide which room to enter. I could have shot him or shot to scare him. But I didn't."

"Drew, you—"

"I'm not finished. He saw me holding the gun and he jumped through the open door into my sister's room. I moved to her door. She awoke and screamed. Again I could have shot him. But I didn't. He hit my sister in the head. Hit her so hard it knocked her out. Then he smashed her window and climbed out. Again, I could have shot him, but I didn't."

"Was your sister okay?"

"She spent several days in the hospital being checked out for head injuries. Eventually, she was okay. But when my grandfather heard the story of what happened, he was livid. He said he'd given me the gun because he thought I was a man. But if I couldn't shoot someone to protect my own sister, then I just didn't have what it takes to be a man. He said people like that never have what it takes. He called me a coward, not even worthy of the West name."

When he stopped talking, tear tracks glistened on Beth's cheeks. She wiped them. "Did—did he ever take back his words?"

"I think he tried to once, but Granddad was stubborn— the John Wayne type that thinks an apology is a sign of weakness."

"How could he say that to his ten-year-old grandson? Didn't he know that was a deep wound that—"

"He didn't care, Beth. So, at age ten, I vowed that no one would ever be able to say that to me again. And anyone in Drew West's charge would be kept safe, no matter the cost to me. I would fight, maim, kill, if necessary, to protect anyone I cared for or thought needed protecting. And I made sure everyone around me knew what to expect if they even acted like they might cross me."

"You became a bully?"

"No. I never bullied people or threatened them to get what I wanted. I just let them know not to mess with me. I never started fights, but I always finished them. And I got called to the principal's office so often you could see the imprint of my rear end in the seat by his desk. Later on, my short fuse almost got me arrested a couple of times."

"Is that why you killed the cartel gunman, the man in the first raft? You shot first, Drew." Her voice grew soft, barely audible.

"No. It wasn't my temper or anything out-of-control that caused me to shoot him. You don't shoot someone God created and made in His own image without a pretty doggoned good reason."

"What reason did he give you?"

"He raised his gun and had his finger on the trigger, but we only had bushes and bunchgrass for shelter. If he'd pulled the trigger, we would have been dead. That's why I shot him. Then Ricardo fired at us. Almost hit us. And so I shot him." He paused. "Now you know all about Drew West, the man who simply isn't adequate, not up to par for a man in the West family."

Beth lifted her head from his shoulder. "Don't say that. It's not true. I wouldn't be alive today if it weren't for you. You took on a man on the FBI's most wanted list. Unarmed, took him down and took away his gun. I don't know anyone who would have even attempted to do that, except maybe my father, and he's dead because of the things he tried. So don't tell me Drew West isn't up to par."

"Thanks for the vote of confidence. I hope you won't regret it."

She laid her head on his shoulder again. "Drew, I heard about the US Marshal protection that the DOJ offered me, and I chose you instead. And I chose based on what I saw you do." Her voice came hardly above a whisper. "That ought to tell you something." She sighed and yawned.

"That's enough about me. You were tired when we drove in. Shouldn't we get some sleep?"

"Uh huh. We ... should." Her long eyelashes tickled his cheek as they fluttered.

"We need to be alert tomorrow. We can't afford to let anyone follow us home, or we won't be safe in Oregon."

She didn't reply.

"Beth, aren't you ready to—"

She snorted, wiggled her mouth and resumed her steady, deep breathing. She had zonked and he was still holding her.

This is exactly what I said I wouldn't do.

But she was tired and sleeping peacefully. He couldn't disturb her.

Drew's mind and body hinted at exhaustion too. Telling his story drained him further. He slid down a bit, slumping on the couch.

Beth's head came with him. It now lay on his chest.

Waking up in the morning could prove interesting. But he was too tired to move.

Drew curled an arm around Beth's shoulders and joined her.

Chapter 12

The day had begun at 6:30 a.m. with a blushing Beth Sanchez in his arms on the couch.

She didn't comment on them falling asleep together. Beth simply got up, got dressed, and they left.

During their six-hundred-mile drive home to Way West Ranch, Beth hadn't talked a tenth as much as in the previous two days, even when they stopped for her to buy a few clothes.

But Drew was not going to complain. She had been glued to his side the entire day. In the truck, when the traffic was light and the road straight—which proved to be about five hundred of the six hundred miles he drove—her hand remained in his.

Drew didn't talk much either. No more marriage proposals, nor references to his premature proposal, and no more predictions of their engagement.

When a beautiful young woman like Beth wants to be close to you, who would be stupid enough to open their mouth and mess everything up?

The closer they got to the ranch, the closer Beth got to him.

As he drove westward down Highway 126 from Redmond toward the ranch, she had one hand on the console to prop herself up and she leaned toward him.

"This is beautiful, Drew. It is a bit like the high desert around my old home in Mexico. But we did not have the volcanic peaks nearby."

"The peak to the north, in the distance, is Mount Jefferson. The three peaks west of us are the Three Sisters. Near the base of those three peaks is the small town of Sisters. It's full of gift shops, restaurants, and some of the best coffee in the state."

Beth's hand clamped onto his arm. "Your mother has no idea I am coming."

Was that why she'd been so quiet? "That's right. We couldn't afford to let anyone know."

"What will she think? I have just traveled half-way across the United States with her son, unchaperoned. What will she think of me?"

"Beth, my mother is going to treat you like her daughter."

"You held me all night last night."

"Yeah. We were exhausted and it was innocent. But you might not want to mention that to my mom."

Beth dipped her head but didn't reply.

"She will love you, Beth. When I explain our circumstances, she'll understand. She knows me and knows that I wouldn't treat any woman dishonorably, though you were at times a big temptation." He grinned.

"That's not funny, Mr. West."

"No it isn't. It was pretty doggoned hard to resist Señorita Sanchez's charms. Then there was that kiss after the pillow fight."

"You cannot tell her about that. About any of it. It was— was out of character for me." Beth's breathing had turned to near panting.

"Relax and just be yourself. You can trust my mom as much as you trust me. She will love you. She won't find fault "

"But you did. You said I was a—"

"And I was joking, wasn't I?"

"I'm sorry. It's just that I didn't think what this moment would be like. It's not just you and me now. There's another person."

"That's not all. My nephew and niece will be here, spending the summer on the ranch."

"How old are they?"

"Melanie—we call her Mel—is eight, maybe nine now. And Cooper—we call him Coop—is ten. Almost eleven."

Drew turned off the highway onto the small paved road that ran by the east entrance to the ranch. "These scattered trees are Juniper trees."

"They don't look like Mexican Juniper trees."

"They're not. I think Mexico has weeping Junipers, bushier. The trees here are taller. We have a river just to the west of the ranch. It's called the Deschutes River. Some of the best steelhead fishing in the world. When we get a chance, I'll take you to see Steelhead Falls."

"But this isn't a vacation. We're running for our lives. We're hiding."

"Yes. But we're hiding in beautiful country. I think it is fitting that a beautiful señorita should see the beautiful scenery as she adds her own beauty to it. Here's the turn-off to the Way West Ranch." He slowed and turned onto the wide gravel road built to accommodate large horse trailers and trucks.

"Is it called Way West because it is so far west?"

"Not really. It's named after a Hollywood movie that was filmed here called *The Way West*. It tells the story of an early wagon train to Oregon. My granddad started the ranch in 1967, the same year the movie released."

"Is that the ranch house?" Beth pointed to the sprawling, one-level house straight ahead.

"That's it. It has over 4,000 square feet of living area. Five bedrooms. Three bathrooms, including the guest bathroom, which will probably be yours, depending on where Mom decided to put Mel and Coop."

Drew parked along the sweeping circle drive that provided access to the house and the barns. "The big barn is where our riding horses and a few of the mares are kept. The mares with foals are in the smaller buildings beyond the barn. It's almost six o'clock and the barn door is open. So Mom is probably feeding horses." He opened the driver's door. "Come on. Let's go tell her we're here."

Beth opened her door. "I am having second thoughts about this."

"That's okay for right now. But let's take care of that before you have any third thoughts."

As they walked to the barn, Beth seemed glued to his side. It was not like her to be shy.

Maybe there was more to it than shyness. Beth hadn't had a family for about eight years. She was about to acquire one again. And the way she lost her family probably had a lot to do with her discomfort.

Drew needed to manage her introduction to ease this transition in her life.

When they walked into the barn, Beth separated from him. She stopped in the doorway, looking like she might turn and run.

The rear-end of a trim and fit middle-aged horse rancher stuck out of one stall beneath the head of a thoroughbred quarter horse.

"Mom, it's Drew."

She turned, dropped a bucket of feed and ran toward him. "Drew, what in the world are you doing here? I thought you'd be off doing research in Texas until August."

She wrapped Drew up in a bear hug.

"Mom, I brought someone with me."

"You know that Hunter's always welcome here, Drew. You don't have to—"

"It's not Hunter."

Beth walked toward them.

His mom took a step back and her eyes widened. Slowly a smile spread across her face. "It's about time. When's the wedding?"

He chose not to reply. Instead, he turned to Beth and mouthed, "Told you so."

"Mom, this is Elizabeth Sanchez. She goes by Beth."

"It's nice to meet you, Mrs. West." Beth took a couple of steps then reached out her hand.

"Beth. I'm Mattie." His mom ignored the hand and stepped in to give Beth the same hug she'd given Drew. "Let me finish feeding this pregnant mare, then you can tell me all about it."

The high-pitched voice of children came through the barn door.

Melanie and Cooper ran into the barn and stopped. Then they sprinted toward Drew and both leaped into his arms.

He caught one with his right hand, the other with his left. "You guys are getting too big for this." Drew set them down and turned them around toward Beth. "I've got someone you need to meet. Mel, Coop, this is Beth. She'll be staying with us."

Mel's mouth dropped open and she stared at Beth for a few seconds. "Is she a Spanish princess?"

"I don't know. Are you, Beth?" Drew said.

Beth met Mel's gaze. "I'm just Beth."

"What's your last name?" Coop said.

"I'm Elizabeth Sanchez, but just call me Beth."

Drew tapped his mother's shoulder. "Mom, when we get a chance, we need to talk. Just the three of us."

She raised her eyebrows. "I heard a rumor that you had borrowed Grant's truck, but no one would tell me much. Is it that bad?"

"Well, it's not good. We'll tell you about it later. But we've been cooped up in the truck all day and need to stretch our legs." He motioned toward the far end of the barn. "Would you like to take a walk, Beth? I can show you our mares and the foals."

"Come on, kids," Mattie said. "Drew and Beth need some time to relax after their long ride. We can visit with them later."

"But I haven't seen Uncle Drew since—"

Mattie gave Coop that look that all mothers seem to have mastered.

"Aw, alright."

Drew walked through the big barn with Beth at his side. They stopped at the far end and looked out across the green pasture lined with white wooden fences.

The sun sat above the Cascade mountains directly in front of them—a tranquil setting that did not reflect the urgency or the danger that had sent Drew and Beth to this ranch.

"Since I'm a business major, I've got to ask this question—you don't have to answer—but, is raising horses a good way to make a living? It seems to me that the costs of all this would be so high that you'd have to sell your horses for a lot of money."

"About the costs, you've got that right. A few years ago a registered foal with the right sire could bring ten to fifteen thousand dollars. But things have changed. We can get three or four thousand for an untrained colt. More for a partially trained one. But older, well-trained horses, with the right credentials, can still bring twenty thousand. And prices vary with the US economy."

"You told me these were equine dragsters. Are they racehorses?"

"Yeah. They run short races. Certainly not the Belmont Stakes. But quarter horses have been clocked at nearly sixty miles-per-hour. They can run the quarter-mile more than twice as fast as Olympic champions. But people use them for rodeo horses—barrel racing and calf roping—for ranch horses, show horses, pleasure riding, some folks even use them for jumping. When you see horses in the movies, odds are they're quarter horses."

"When I look across the pasture at all the horses, I can't believe all the colors."

"Yep. You'll see bays, blacks, brown horses, buckskins, a few palominos, grays, and duns come in several colors as do the roans." Drew paused. "Your ancestors helped start this breed, Beth. Most believe the quarter horse is a cross between the Spanish horses brought to the New World and those brought in by the American colonists."

"Papa would have loved to see this." She swiped at an eye.

Drew noticed and stepped closer.

"I'm okay, Drew. We probably should have that talk with your mother. She needs to know about the trouble I'm bringing."

"That's not all on your shoulders. Suarez wants me just as badly ... if not more. You should have seen that look in his eyes after I took him down and got his gun."

"I did see. And it frightened me so much I almost got sick."

"Well, let's go have that chat with Mom and make some contingency plans in case Suarez were to locate us. He doesn't have freedom to roam the US, so it's not likely he'll find us. And he can't waltz in here with his army."

"He has his ways, Drew. We dare not underestimate him."

When Beth and Drew walked into the ranch house through the kitchen door, Mattie, Coop, and Mel sat around the kitchen table eating what looked like berry cobbler.

"Mom, we should have that conversation now."

"Kids, eat your cobbler here. I need to talk with your uncle. I won't be long. If you get bored, you can watch TV in the den."

The three walked through a wide doorway into a rustic living room with furniture constructed from hand-hewn pine. Mattie and Beth sat on the couch and Drew pulled up a chair on the other side of the coffee table.

"Here's what we're facing, Mom." He described the situation with Suarez, explaining why the man wanted Beth and why he wanted Drew.

His mother waited patiently until he finished. There was no panic or alarm, only a deep concern in her eyes that now focused on him. "Drew, I told you all that fighting was going to get you in trouble someday."

"Mom, what was I supposed to do? Let them kill Beth?"

"Easy, son. I see you've still got that hair trigger."

Beth gave him a frown and nodded.

"Rather than play beat up on Drew, shouldn't we be planning what we'll do if Suarez discovers that Beth and I have come to the ranch?"

Mattie nodded. "I'll need to take Mel and Coop somewhere. There are several places we can go, but let me think about that for a bit. What about you and Beth?"

"I was thinking about hiding out in the old cabin until law enforcement intervenes."

Beth had been silent through most of the conversation. She sat up on the couch. "When he came to our town, he surprised us in the middle of the night. Whatever plan we choose, we must be ready in case he surprises us."

"Beth, Agent Preston said he'd monitor FBI Intelligence and give us a call if Suarez makes a move this direction."

"Now do you see why I was hesitant to come here, Drew. We can't endanger your mother and the children."

"You didn't seem too hesitant when you told Whittaker where to get off."

"Coming with you and coming here are two different considerations."

Mattie studied Beth's face. "I see. If coming with Drew was your first consideration, maybe there *is* a wedding on the horizon."

"I asked her, Mom."

Beth's eyes widened. "The same day you met me."

"It seemed appropriate."

Mattie shook her head. "That's Drew, always—"

"Always storming the castle?" Beth said.

Mattie laughed. "Bet you got that from Hunter."

"Yes. But he's right. Your son storms castles and takes whatever he wants."

"You haven't tried very hard to stop me, Beth."

"But if we're not alive, none of that matters."

"Mom, maybe you should make some calls tonight and make sure Mel and Coop keep their bags packed. If there's any possibility of danger, the minute we hear of it, you take the four-by-four and leave the ranch by the back road. Beth and I will keep some things packed and be ready to go. We can take the truck or even take two horses to get away into the hills and work our way over to the cabin above Steelhead Falls."

Beth blew out a sharp sigh. "Drew, the plan sounds good to you because you haven't seen what Suarez can do. He brought an army to our town, surrounded it, and no one got away."

"But Suarez can't sneak an army into the US? He'd be stopped. I say we go with our plan and be ready to execute it at a moment's notice."

Beth laid her hand on his arm. "I hope you're right, Drew. Because if you're wrong, I couldn't live with myself."

He looked down at the hand on his arm. "If I'm wrong, you wouldn't have to."

Chapter 13

Today I'm going horseback riding.

Beth's heart was thumping out a presto rhythm as she studied the two horses Drew led out of the barn, one red the other light brown.

She bounced on her toes like an excited schoolgirl. When Beth looked at Drew, she couldn't suppress a giggle.

He glanced at her feet and grinned. "Yeah. Horses can do that to a person."

"What are their names?"

"The buckskin is Dusty, and the red roan is Sundown. Some folks call her a strawberry roan."

Her gaze locked on the big horse. No matter what angle Beth looked at the horse, its coat seemed to glow red around the edges of its profile. "I like Sundown."

"Good choice." He circled Beth, pulled her hand behind her back, and placed something cold and wet in it.

She gasped.

"It's just a carrot. Horse candy. Feed it to her and she'll be your friend for life."

"So Sundown's a girl?"

"More like a middle-aged woman."

Beth rubbed the front of Sundown's head then presented the carrot.

Sundown's muzzle swept across her hand and the carrot was gone. In a couple of seconds, the muzzle returned, seeking Beth's hand again.

"Oh, all right. This was supposed to be Dusty's." Drew gave Beth another carrot.

The carrot disappeared, and Sundown crunched on it for a few seconds then nodded her head in approval and snorted.

"Horses can eat a lot of treats, but you never want to give them a stimulant, like caffeine. They already push the limits of their hearts when they run. A stimulant could push them beyond the limits."

"It could cause a heart attack?"

"More like heart burst ... or arrythmia."

Beth rubbed Sundown's muzzle. "I guess you'll just have breakfast without coffee."

Drew handed her the reins. "She's gentle and usually knows what you want to do before you do."

"Like a certain man I know."

"Could be. The only thing that scares her is rattlesnakes."

"That's something Sundown and I have in common. Any of those where we're going?"

"Probably not. But you never know in the desert."

She mounted Sundown and tested the stirrups with her feet.

Drew nodded his approval of her mounting Sundown, then watched Beth for a moment. His gaze swept down from her face to the stirrups. It stopped near her right foot. "How's your ankle?"

"It doesn't hurt unless I try to run on it or bend it too far."

"Think you can put enough weight on it to stand on your stirrups while the horse is moving?"

"It will be fine. But ... Drew, this is more than just a pleasure ride, isn't it?"

Drew swung up into the saddle on Dusty. "Yeah. That's why Mom wouldn't let Mel and Coop come with us ... that and a couple of other reasons." He gave her his warm, winning smile.

"I see."

"Mom likes you, Beth. A lot. I've never brought a girl home before."

"That's hard to believe. Not even in high school?"

"Nope."

"Didn't girls like you? I would have thought you'd have several—"

"Oh, several girls liked me. But think about it. Would you let your daughter date a guy who'd beat up nearly every boy in school? One who had, deservedly or not, acquired a reputation as a hot-tempered ruffian? Well, that's a slight exaggeration. I never did beat up Hunter."

"One who proposes to girls on the first date? Certainly not."

"Only to the right one."

"How do you know it was the right one, Drew?"

"She's the only one you've ever really wanted and the one you know is going to say yes."

"And how do you know this?"

"Because I can read her mind."

The tingling between her shoulder blades brought a shiver and the eerie thought that Drew had told her the truth.

Drew shook the reins and Dusty started off down a dirt road that bypassed the bright green pastures.

Sundown followed without any urging.

The small road headed westward toward the back of the ranch. Miles beyond the ranch, the Cascade Mountains rose to gleaming white peaks against a powder-blue summer sky containing a few puffy white clouds near the mountains.

"This seems like a pleasure ride. What else are we going to do?"

"If we have to run and hide, I want you to be familiar with the area. You'll be safer that way."

"But I'll have you with me, Drew."

"Who knows, I might sprain an ankle or something." He grinned.

"You're not funny. And you don't have sexy ankles."

"Maybe not. But my ankle bones are humongous. That's what you get for being a long jumper who's too lazy to rake the pit."

"I don't get the connection."

"It's a bone density thing—never mind. How good are you at galloping?"

"Not very good. But I bet Sundown is."

"So you'll gallop with me to the end of the fence?"

"Is this a test or something?"

"Beth Sanchez doesn't miss much, does she?"

"I'd miss *you* if you sprained your ankle."

"But would you miss me if Dusty galloped away leaving you and Sundown in the dust?"

When Drew took off on Dusty, Sundown didn't need a nudge or a kick to get going.

The exhilaration of being carried along by a half-ton running machine sent Beth on a power trip. Why did cars need three-hundred horsepower, when one horsepower could do this?

She almost kicked Sundown to break into a run and pass Drew, but a video played in her mind of Beth falling off an equine dragster and her body bouncing down the dusty road. It wasn't a pretty picture.

She relaxed and moved with the horse as it loped down the road behind Dusty and Drew.

Drew pulled on the reins and Dusty slowed to a trot.

Before Beth could react, Sundown had slowed and soon fell into a walk beside Dusty.

Drew looked her way and studied her face for a moment. "Pretty cool, huh? Almost makes you want to give her a kick and see how fast a quarter horse can go."

"Yes, it does." He'd done it again. Once or twice and she might have called it coincidence or a logical deduction. But Drew had read her mind at least a dozen times since they met.

He pointed to a ridge about a mile ahead. "We will climb over the shoulder of that hill, cross the ridge using that little saddle, and then circle that small peak to a spot a little below the top. Nestled in the trees is a log cabin with most of the conveniences of home. But it's missing a few. There are no roads in, only a small trail for horses or hikers. We don't allow motorcycles or ATVs up there. Too much of a fire hazard."

A half-hour later, Beth dismounted Sundown near the door of the cabin.

The cabin faced west only a short way from the top of the ridge. The setting provided a spectacular view of the Cascade Mountains.

Drew worked an old pump handle until water poured out into a trough. He pumped for a while, then they tethered both horses to a rail beside the watering trough.

"While they drink, I'm going to show you our cabin."

"*Our* cabin? Do you own this? I mean it's a long way from the ranch."

"My grandfather built it. Mom and Dad added some amenities, and it is actually in my name. It could be our cabin, Beth." He smiled.

She didn't.

But Drew had added another line item to Drew West's balance sheet in the assets column that had formed in Beth's MBA mind. And saying no to him, which had been her intent on day one, was ... well, on day five, she wouldn't bet money on a horse with such long odds. But none of this speculation mattered if they couldn't stay away from Suarez and stay alive.

Drew pulled out his keys, unlocked the cabin, and motioned her inside. "It's a two-bedroom home away from home. Has a good well, but you have to pump the water from either the kitchen sink or the pump outside. The only other drawbacks are the outhouse and no electricity."

"Drew, this is wonderful. And in this setting, it would be a great place for—"

"For a honeymoon ..."

"Are you asking or making a statement?"

"I've already asked, Beth. So, I guess I was making a statement."

She couldn't think of a good reply. Besides they were checking the cabin out as a hiding place, not a honeymoon cottage.

"As a hideout, this spot is hidden from view of anyone coming from the ranch." He paused. "As a honeymoon cottage, this spot is hidden from view of anyone coming from the ranch."

"You've made your point, Drew. Let's focus on the hideout because ... if that doesn't work, there will never be a honeymoon cottage."

"You sure like to flirt with ideas, concepts, and people, but you're really slow at commitment, Beth Sanchez. Did you know that?"

"Not if I know I'm right. If I'm certain, I can commit in a few seconds. That's a characteristic of all INTJs."

"So if I told you I was Mr. Right, you would have said yes that first day?"

"No. You have to *be* it not *tell* it."

"Kind of like writing fiction? Showing instead of telling?"

"I don't know anything about writing fiction. But that sounds right."

"Back to the advantages of this cabin. A person would have to cross the ridgeline in the right spot or they wouldn't find the cabin. And for someone hiding here, they can climb about fifty yards to the top of the ridge and see anybody approaching from the east for at least fifteen miles. And right from the cabin window we can see thirty miles to the west. What do you think?"

"I love it here. But suppose, somehow, Suarez found us. What would we do?"

"Let's mount up and I'll show you."

It took them nearly a half-hour to ride down from the ridge to a road near the river. A mile down the road they came to a graveled parking area surrounded by pine trees.

"This is the Steelhead Falls trailhead. The trail to the falls has some steep spots where steps have been cut into the ground, and there are steep side slopes that I don't want to take the horses down. If you took a spill, we could lose you, the horse, or both. You and the horse would both have to be airlifted out, and I would have to pay for it. We'll hitch Dusty and Sundown here and walk in. It's only about a half mile to the falls."

"What happens if—"

"I figured you'd ask that. If we're followed to the falls, I'll show you after we get there."

They hitched their horses to the post at the trailhead and Drew led the way down a dusty trail that followed the east side of a dry desert canyon bordered by rock walls. Soon the rocks towered a hundred feet or more above them.

The rush of water echoed off the canyon walls. The Deschutes, a blue ribbon which turned white where the water tumbled over rocks, was a stream of life running through an otherwise arid land.

Streams in the Desert. That was a devotional she'd read while in college. We wait on God. He waits on us and works out His purposes in our lives.

Was Drew part of God's purposes in Beth's life? Maybe Drew was a stream bringing life to the desolate existence Beth had suffered through for the past eight years. The bit of life she'd experienced with Drew was real and vibrant, despite the threat of death at the hands of that demon, Hector Suarez.

And in a few moments, Beth would see a real stream in the desert. Decisions about the reality of Drew West bringing life to the desert of her life would have to wait.

Insufficient data. One never should make a decision without enough data points to validate it.

Almost a half mile down the trail, the side slope became so steep that the trail angled sharply downhill. Each step required Beth's ankle to hold the weight of her body while the ankle bent to the right.

She grimaced after a couple of steps as pain stabbed her ankle and the side of her foot.

Beth stopped on the trail, hoping the pain would subside, but Drew had already stepped off the trail and positioned his body below hers.

"I'm sorry, Beth. I'd forgotten how steep the slope is. Put your hand on top of my shoulder and lean on me. It'll take the weight off your ankle."

"Thanks."

In five steps, which held much less pain, Beth passed the steep side slope.

They emerged from behind a rock outcropping and the falls roared through the canyon below them.

Beth stopped on the trail and soaked in the beauty of Steelhead Falls.

The river dropped a dozen feet or more, and the rock cliff forming the falls divided the river into five different white cascades. The largest two cascades sent spray into the brilliant sunlight, creating rainbows that shimmered as the water droplets drifted in the gentle breeze.

"Drew, this is absolutely spectacular."

"Come on. You ain't seen nothin' yet." He took her hand and led Beth down to a large rock that jutted out into the river.

When they reached the outer edge of the rock and then turned to face the falls, it seemed that Beth stood in the middle of the river looking back at the falls.

The river roared and rushed straight at them. Rainbows came and went at the whims of the sun and the breeze. A fine mist reached them, partially cooling Drew and Beth from the sun which had turned scorching over the past hour.

Beth stretched out her arms and turned a full circle in the mist. "If only I could come here every day."

"That can be arranged, Ms. Sanchez. But, first, you need to become Mrs. West."

"No, Drew. First we need to resolve a minor problem we both have called Hector Suarez."

"I handled Suarez once and I'll do it again. He won't hurt you, Beth. Nobody gets through me to hurt someone I love."

Drew stopped talking after his use of a certain four-letter word. Evidently, he realized this was the first time either of them had used the word in reference to the other.

She chose not to mention his premature admission. "Drew, that's what my father thought because he drove out Suarez. It looked like it was true, for a while. Then ..."

"Like I said, I handled him once and—"

"He won't underestimate you this time."

"Do you think that's why I took him down and took his gun?"

"No. You had the ability to do it. But if he had known that, he might have killed you before you had a chance. He's evil, demonic "

"Now you're touching upon his real weakness."

"What do you mean?"

"You said he's demonic. What do we have going for us that Hector does not?"

"You mean God?"

"Exactly. I can guarantee you that Hector Suarez underestimates God one-hundred percent of the time."

Beth couldn't hold back a laugh. "You're right. We stand here planning how we can survive Hector Suarez, and we know that, ultimately, Hector's the one who won't survive."

Sometime during their exchange, Drew's arm had curled around her waist. "Beth, when this is all over and behind us, I'll need to know the answer to my question."

"You didn't phrase it as a question, Drew. Marry me. That's a command."

"Well I meant it as a question, and I'll need an answer."

"I know." She clasped her hands behind Drew's neck and pulled him closer until there was no other option but to kiss him.

"That's the second time you've kissed me, Beth. Is the third time going to be the charm? Or can you give me an answer now?"

"I'm not ready to say yes. But, Drew ... I want you to know that I'm not saying no."

"Gee. After five whole days, is that all you can tell me?"

* * *

I want you to know that I'm not saying no.

To get that bit of an admission from Beth Sanchez— Drew considered it a major victory. It sent his spirit soaring. He couldn't keep a smile off his face as he recalled Beth's words.

Those words had almost made him forget the reason they had gone on this expedition. He wasn't through yet finding a path of escape should the drug lord discover he and Beth were at Way West Ranch. And he had forgotten to show Beth the cave across the river from the falls. That could wait.

As they climbed the last hill that would take them back to the trailhead, Sundown whinnied.

Beth pointed at the horse and smiled.

"Yeah. She knows it's you," Drew said. "A horse never forgets a friend, especially if they bring carrots."

"How does she know it's me?"

"She can see you, and her eyesight is better than yours, even if she is fifty-five in horse years. Now that the valleys are heating, the wind has reversed. It's blowing up the canyons, so she can smell you too."

"How can I tell her I like her?"

"Talk softly to her. Be gentle. And, of course, give her treats."

"But I don't have anything to give her."

Beth and Drew walked side-by-side through the gate at the trailhead. Drew stopped beside Dusty and shoved a hand into the saddle pack.

His hand came out palming a small paper package. Drew ripped it open.

Beth had stopped beside him, and she stuck out a hand when she saw the label, sugar cubes.

He dropped a cube into her palm. "You can't make this a habit. It's not good for them to have too much sugar."

Beth circled in front of Dusty, then moved in front of Sundown and rubbed her head. She put the back of her hand near the horse's mouth.

Sundown took in a breath, then she used her nose to nudge Beth's hand upward.

"Guess I can't fool you. You knew it was there." She opened her hand, palm up, and the sugar cube disappeared.

The horse's nose searched Beth's hand.

"Sorry, girl, that's all for now." She turned toward Drew. "Where to now?"

"You asked where we'd go if they discovered us at Steelhead Falls. That's where we're headed."

"Then why did we—"

"We're taking an alternate route, so we can ride the horses to this place. I thought you might like that better than walking on a sore ankle."

"Be careful, Drew. You might turn into a thoughtful alpha male. You might even forget how to storm castles."

"I just thought that, since you and Sundown have bonded, you might like to ride to pine tree valley."

"That's what I was talking about."

"You mcan mе being thoughtful? Giving you and Sundown some more bonding time?"

She nodded.

"Beth, when someone lowers the drawbridge for you, you don't have to storm the castle. Besides, I'm already inside." He slid into the saddle.

Beth's cheeks turned pink as she mounted Sundown.

Why was it embarrassing for her to admit she had feelings for him? Maybe that was part of being one of those INTJ women.

He pointed to the south. "Let's go upstream. There's a shallow rapids where we can ford the river. We'll cross into the next valley, and it'll take us back to a point west of the falls. From there we go up into a valley filled with pine trees."

Drew's cell buzzed and music played.

Beth looked around them, then focused on Drew. "What's that?"

"My cell." He pulled it from his pocket.

"What was it playing?"

"Peter's theme, you know, from Peter and the Wolf. Means it's Hunter. I'd better see what he has for us."

"This is Drew."

"Hey, bro, how're things going with you and Beth?"

"Fine. Now, why did you really call?"

"That FBI agent, Preston, called me."

"Did he have a message for me?"

"Sort of. I think, mainly, he wanted you to know that he's still monitoring intel on the Del Rio Cartel."

"But did he have any info?"

"He just said there were indications Hector Suarez might be getting ready to take a trip. He'll keep watching and let you know if Suarez makes a move."

"That's it? Suarez looks restless, like maybe he's going on a trip?"

Beth's gaze focused on Drew's face and the twin frown lines on her forehead deepened.

"That's it. Are you making any plans in case you need to move?"

"Yeah. We're making plans."

"Take care, bro. I'll be in touch." Hunter ended the call.

"Drew, what's happening with Suarez?"

He slid his cell into his pocket. "My guess is that the intel was inconclusive, but Agent Preston's gut tells him Suarez is getting ready to make a move. He just couldn't say that officially. So he gave us a subtle warning."

"Do we need to do anything differently?"

Drew nudged Dusty. The horse turned and headed up the road that followed the river.

Beth brought Sundown alongside. "Well, what do you think?"

"The only difference that call makes is that we need to make sure Mom finds a place for all the horses, pronto. Right now, you and I just need to check out this valley and plan how we would retreat further west if Suarez tracked us to the river."

Twenty minutes later, they had forded the river, climbed the ridge on the west side of the Deschutes and crossed the ridgeline using a deep saddle.

Drew studied the long valley as they descended into it. "We had a wet winter and a fairly wet spring. But since then, nothing."

"You'd never guess that on the other side of the ridge is a river lined with all kinds of green vegetation. This looks almost as dry as the desert where I came from in Mexico."

He nudged Dusty. "Let's pick up the pace a little. We need to check out this valley hiding place and then get back to the ranch."

"Should you call your mom now, Drew?"

"I don't want to tell her about Hunter's call over the phone. I want to see her eyes when we talk about it. If she's worried that we can't place all the horses, it'll show in her eyes, not her voice."

"Are you always so calculating? You aren't always processing information, are you?"

Drew turned in the saddle and met her gaze. "It's more like receiving information. Shall I tell you what you're thinking right now?"

"No." She looked away and mumbled something obviously not intended for his ears, something he couldn't understand.

In another ten minutes, they reached the mouth of the small valley filled with many thick stands of pine trees.

"If we're chased this far, we'll go up this valley to where it dead-ends against a rock cliff just below the top of the ridge at the west end."

"A box canyon? Wouldn't we be trapped?"

"No, I'm counting on this canyon buying us some time to get further away to the west. Once we're out of this canyon, if we have to, we can keep going west all the way to the Cascade Mountains. The Cascades are high mountains. Snow covered. Capped with glaciers. It's dangerous to go wandering if you don't know what you're doing."

"And you do?"

"Beth, I don't think even a vindictive man like Suarez could follow us into those mountains. I almost wish he would try. It might get him killed. But, yeah, I can take care of us up there."

Drew moved Dusty into the lead as their path grew narrow while they wound through the pine trees.

"See that cliff ahead?"

"Yes, but what do we do when we reach it? It looks more than a hundred feet high."

"Prepare to be amazed."

"You don't have to keep trying to impress me, Mr. West." She gave him her enigmatic smile.

"I'm not. I'm trying to depress Hector Suarez. I'll show you how in a minute or two."

After they reached the rock cliff that surrounded them on three sides, Drew dismounted. "Come on. Let me show you around."

Beth climbed out of her saddle and stood beside Sundown.

"We can leave the horses here. They won't go anywhere." Drew hurried around the corner of a protruding boulder.

"Wait for me, Drew."

Her footsteps sounded through the opening in the rocks. "Drew? Drew? Where are you?"

The scraping of shoes on rock came through the crack in the rock where Drew stood. "Ouch! That blasted rock!"

A loud thump sounded. "Ouch! This isn't funny, Drew West. Where are you?"

"Right here." He slipped out of the crack then stepped out from behind the rock hiding the entrance.

"You didn't know where I went, and you couldn't find me, right?"

"I scraped my arm trying to climb this boulder and now my toe hurts."

"That's because you got mad at a rock and kicked it."

She folded her arms and didn't reply.

"Let me show you where I was."

"Is there a hidden cave somewhere around here?"

"There's something better. Suarez could trap us in a cave. Follow me."

Drew led her around the big boulder and then slipped behind the huge chunk of rock, shaped like a giant domino, that had fallen into the opening to the crack.

"From here it looks like you're at a dead end. But watch." He slid his body through the narrow gap behind the domino and disappeared.

"How did you—"

"Come on in, Beth."

She followed him into the split in the rocky crown that topped the ridge.

"This split goes through to the other side of the ridge. If we're followed into the box canyon, we just have to beat them to this opening and go through to the other side. Then we head west to the mountains."

"If he knows we disappeared in this canyon, he would keep looking—"

"He would. It could be hours before he found the opening to the crack, if he ever did. By then we'd be climbing glaciers in the Cascades."

Beth craned her neck and looked up to the narrow band of blue sky directly above them. "This is creepy. It's only three or four feet wide. I'd hate to be in here during an earthquake."

"Or an avalanche."

"Avalanche? What do you mean, Drew?"

"From the other side you can walk up to the top. It's littered with rocks two or three feet in diameter. We could bombard anyone coming through the split. We would have them at our mercy. Then we could really give them a headache."

"No, Drew. That's too risky. We should just go to the mountains."

"You're probably right. But it sure is tempting."

They walked through the split and climbed to the pinnacle of the rocky ridge.

Drew pointed to the southeast. "That's Paulina Peak nearly sixty miles away. It sits above two beautiful lakes. Directly south of us, that big peak, nearly ten-thousand feet high, is Mount Bachelor. To the west of us are the Three Sisters. Look up to the north. That perfectly shaped volcanic peak is Mount Jefferson."

"I love this country already, Drew. It's a little like the high desert where I grew up in Mexico, but even more beautiful with these mountains. Best of all, no drug cartels."

"Uh ... that's not the case here in Central Oregon. Drug cartels use Highway 97, the main north-south route on this side of the mountains, to run their drugs through Oregon into Washington and up into Canada."

"Which cartel does that?"

"Authorities think it's the revived Tijuana Cartel, but no one seems to know for sure who runs it." Drew pointed down the rocky slope they had climbed. "We should head back before Sundown gets our horses into mischief."

"Sundown? I think you mean Dusty."

"Sticking up for Sundown? Am I losing my woman to a horse?"

"I don't know. Who's your woman?" She raised her eyebrows and waited.

"My woman knows who she is. But a horse like Sundown is tough competition. However ... when it comes to kissing, I've definitely got an edge over old slobber face."

It looked like Beth tried to keep it in, but the laugh exploded from her mouth, leaving her mouth looking like old slobber face.

She wiped her mouth and regained her composure.

If only their time together was free from concern about Suarez. Drew's time with Beth was fun and exciting, a salve to his scarred soul. No. It made the wounds from his past irrelevant. As if they'd never happened.

When the time was right, he would explain to her how she had healed him. If she cared for him as much as he had begun to care for her, his story might make a difference. And, as she had admitted on their trip from Texas, he had helped her too.

His future looked bright with Beth in it. Holding onto Beth and holding onto life had become synonymous. Without her, he wasn't sure that Drew West wanted a future.

It took an hour to get back to the river and ford it. They'd spent more time on the west side of the river than Drew expected. "Let's take this shortcut back to the ranch. It's a smooth dirt road. The horses will appreciate it."

"Where does this road go."

"It was probably made for access to somebody's homestead a long time ago. People riding motorcycles and ATVs still use it for access to the back country. Hunters use it during deer season."

The road widened about a mile from the county road that led to the ranch. In a turnout along the road, an older sedan sat, inclined to one side.

Drew nodded toward the car. "Somebody has a flat tire. Maybe they need some help."

Three young men got out of the car and looked their way.

Beth pulled Sundown to a stop. "Drew, let's circle around them. We could cut through the field and—"

"It's okay, Beth. People help people out here."

"I don't think we should. I don't like the looks of them."

Chapter 14

"Drew, please? Can we just keep riding?" The three men had a familiar look, one that Beth had seen in the demeanor of cartel drug runners. Men without scruples or honor. Men who tried to take what they wanted.

Right now, the three were looking at her with far too much interest.

"They obviously don't know how to change their tire." Drew said. "Around here, we don't leave people stranded out in the boonies. I'll just give them a hand for a minute, and then we'll go."

He gave her his horses reins and climbed out of the saddle.

"Hey, dude," the tall skinny guy said. "You know how to jack this car up without damaging it?"

"I can probably figure it out. Let me see what you have for a jack and get out your spare tire."

"Here's the lug wrench," the tall guy said.

"She's a hot little jalapeno." The short guy with a smirk on his face stared brazenly at Beth.

"Where did you pick up the illegal? In the Tijuana red-light district?" The one who looked like a football linebacker took a step her way.

Drew laid down the lug wrench and turned to face the two. "You guys need to learn how to conduct yourselves in the presence of a lady. I'm sure she'll overlook your crudeness this time if you apologize to her."

"Apologize? Ain't gonna happen, dude. And ya' wanna know what you can do with your apology?"

This was getting entirely out of hand. "We should go, Drew."

The linebacker picked up the lug wrench like he intended to use it as a club.

Drew motioned Beth to ride her horse to the other side of the road, out of reach of any of the men. But he didn't join her. "Put down the wrench and apologize to the lady."

The short guy laughed.

The lug-wrench linebacker chuckled. "I'm going to tell you what I plan to do with this lug wrench and then what I plan to do to that hot little—"

"It's your funeral, dufus." The ferocity in Drew's eyes frightened Beth.

But the three men didn't seem intimidated, though he now had their full attention.

She had seen Drew in this posture when he'd taken on Suarez. Drew was going to fight them.

If it turned ugly, would he have to kill them? She couldn't let that happen.

"No, Drew." Beth turned her horse, intending to ride between them and break things up before any fighting started.

Before she could turn her horse, Drew kicked the man holding the wrench.

He dropped to the ground and didn't move.

Drew's movement continued after the kick. He punched the other crude commenter.

Blood splattered across the man's face. And his hands went to his nose.

The third young man, the tall skinny one, held both hands out toward Drew in surrender. "Sorry. Didn't mean to offend you."

"Yes, you did." Drew planted a foot in the man's midsection. The kick sent him to the ground, wheezing as he tried to regain the breath Drew had knocked out of him.

"I hope you three learned a lesson about real ladies and real men, because you guys are neither. I'm not sure what we should call boys like you." Drew turned to walk away.

The first man he kicked rolled over and pulled out a knife.

"Drew, watch out!" Beth's horse reared up. She shifted her weight to stay in the saddle and hang onto the reins of Dusty.

The man with the knife lunged toward Drew's back.

Drew whirled and, in one smooth motion, grabbed the wrist of the knife hand, slung the man over Drew's shoulder, and slammed him on the ground with a sickening thud.

Except for his groaning mouth, the man didn't move.

"Stop it, Drew! Let's go!"

He ignored her plea. Instead, Drew glared at the guy who hadn't joined the fight. "You know what's going to happen to you in a few minutes?"

The guy's wide eyes said he'd gotten an inkling.

"They're going to beat the living crud out of you because you bailed on them. Saves me the trouble." Finally, Drew walked her way.

He mounted Dusty.

She tossed him the reins. "You didn't have to do that."

He didn't reply. His eyes still held the furious look they'd maintained during the fight. He stared at the road ahead of them and didn't look her way.

"Drew, there was no need for any violence. You could have avoided it."

"No one who threatens you is going to get away with it, Beth. And they talked like they were going to try to make good on those threats."

"Don't make this about me. It's about you losing your temper and using your fighting skills against people who can't even—"

"What did you want me to do, Beth. Wait until one of them pulled out a gun?" He blew out a blast of air. "Look, when anybody threatens someone I'm protecting, they are going to suffer the consequences, every time."

"I'm not your little sister and you're not ten years old."

His eyes flashed anger that was now directed at her. "Guess I won't be trusting you with any more of my personal history, not if you're going to—"

"I'm sorry. I just wanted to make my point."

"You made it, Beth."

Though Drew needed to hear those words, for his own sake, Beth wanted them back. She should never have taken a sore spot on Drew's heart and ripped off the scabs.

"But I wish I hadn't. I'm sorry, Drew. Look at me, please?"

He blew out a sharp sigh and made eye contact. "I'm sorry too."

"So where do we go from here?"

She wasn't sure, and Drew didn't reply.

Chapter 15

Was Ramon neglecting his duties? There had been no confirmation of Mr. West's and Ms. Sanchez's arrival or presence at that ranch in Oregon.

Suarez sat on the couch in his suite inside his compound with his finger hovering over the call icon for Ramon's cell phone. Hector could take no definitive action until he was sure of the location of the two targets.

He cursed and pressed the icon.

"Suarez, I was about to call you."

"What a coincidence, a convenient coincidence."

Ramon didn't reply.

"Have you seen them, Ramon?"

"A few minutes ago, they rode two horses down the long driveway and then took their horses to the barn."

"So they are enjoying their little love affair while I hobble around on a knee that is barely functional."

"I do not think they are enjoying it too much. From this distance, I could not be sure, but they were not, how do you say it, *íntimamente*?"

"Perhaps it was a lovers' quarrel. Anything that distracts them is to our advantage. Well, they are at the ranch, so I am leaving for Tijuana."

"Tijuana? Are you sure you can trust them, Hector? How do we know you will come back alive?"

"I will be safe. Besides our gentlemen's agreement, I am bringing twenty men with me. They are already across the border and have transportation to our destination. They are my insurance, Ramon."

"Who is this man in Tijuana that you are trusting so much?"

"That is not a good question to ask. In usual circumstances, it might endanger you. But, in this case, perhaps you should know. His name is Luis Santana."

"I have never heard of him."

"That is good. But I'm afraid Luis will not enjoy his anonymity for long. His organization is growing, but we are not yet competitors. Hopefully, this cooperation will maintain our friendship, which is advantageous to both of us."

"I do not mean to question your judgment, Hector, but how is that to both of our advantages?"

"Luis wants to know more about how we eliminated the resistors in Laguna. I help them implement a plan to eliminate resistance in their area, and they help me on this venture. I will also help them stop the Zetas from encroachment into Tijuana territory."

Ramon was silent for a moment. "But you are already talking to Los Zetas about a non-interference agreement."

"I am not willing to start a war with the Zetas on behalf of the Tijuana cartel. Any agreement with the Zetas, even a verbal agreement between us and them, is enough to say that I have kept my promise to Luis Santana."

"Even if it does not protect the Tijuana Cartel?"

"As long as I can spin it sufficiently to satisfy Luis, yes."

"I hope Luis doesn't—"

"And that, Ramon, is why you cannot express any knowledge of any agreements between cartels. You may encounter Luis's men while we are in Oregon. One remark from you can destroy what I have spent months building. You would be punished accordingly for such a mistake."

"I know nothing of inter-organizational agreements, Hector. I am simply your personal private detective."

"Well said, my friend."

"Have you talked with Ricardo or his lawyer?"

"No. But I expect a call from his lawyer tomorrow or the next day. Ricardo isn't as weak as you think, Ramon. He will survive prison for a few weeks."

"When can I expect to see you here?"

"Lopez is flying me to Juarez. But my commercial flight from Juarez arrives in the middle of the night in Tijuana. Then we leave immediately for Oregon. You should see me in three days max. Maybe sooner. Keep watching them, Ramon. We need to know what they do and when, and where they go in the local area. Once I arrive, we need to strike quickly. And no building, no animal and no person there can be allowed to survive."

Chapter 16

Beth had been a no-show at breakfast. After their disagreement yesterday, it wasn't a good sign.

Did she really believe he was too volatile and violent to be around? That he wouldn't make a good husband or father, because he was determined to stop evil people with violence if they wouldn't listen to words?

He and Beth needed to talk. But would she?

About 9:00 a.m. she had slipped out the door and went to the barn. Probably to see Sundown. But she'd been out there over an hour.

Maybe Drew should try to talk to her in the barn. Being with the horses might help his cause.

The back door opened, and Beth entered the dining room. She stopped when she saw Drew sitting at the table with Mel and Cooper.

Drew stood. "Beth—"

The ranch phone rang. The old ringer jangled his nerves and stopped his words. Something about the call, maybe its timing, seemed ominous, like some evil force driving a wedge between Beth and him.

Beth's eyes, darting between him and the phone, said she also had concerns about the call.

"I'll get it," Coop said. "It might be Mom." He answered the phone, then his eyebrows rose, and his mouth dropped open. "Just a minute, sir ... Uncle Drew, it's an FBI agent and he wants to talk to you."

Mattie entered from the kitchen. She studied Drew's face for a moment. "What's wrong?"

"Mom, would you please take the kids to the kitchen. Get them some desert or something."

She nodded. "Coop, Mel, there's still some cobbler left. Let's have some."

Coop handed Drew the phone and followed his grandmother out of the room.

Drew blew out a breath and lifted the phone to his ear. "This is Drew."

"Agent Tom Preston, here. I talked to your friend, Hunter Jones, and he reluctantly gave me this number."

"Yeah. We knew at some point you would need to know exactly where we were. But what's up?"

"I've been talking to an analyst in the FBI Intelligence Branch. Reports indicate that some members of the Del Rio Cartel crossed the Mexican border into California. We believe they're traveling with, and possibly collaborating with, members of the Tijuana Cartel."

"What do you make of that, Preston?"

"These are, for the most part, noncompeting crime organizations. So cooperation as a reason for traveling together, while unusual, can't be ruled out. We know the Tijuana cartel moves drugs north to Oregon along both the I-5 and Highway 97 corridors."

"What do you think they're up to?"

"This is speculation, so we could be wrong. But we think they're forming a small army, a tactical operations group. Other members of Del Rio entered the US, near El Paso, a couple of days ago. We believe they plan to come after you and Ms. Sanchez. That would fit with the way Hector Suarez has operated in the past. Up until now, his violent activities have been confined to Northeastern Mexico. But with what just happened in Florence ADX—"

"What do you mean? What just happened?"

"Ricardo Suarez was nearly killed in a fight at the federal penitentiary in Florence, Colorado yesterday. He's listed as critical."

"So you think that pushed Suarez over the edge far enough to plan an attack in the US?"

"That's exactly what we think. The people who spotted the Tijuana members working with Suarez are sure they detected Elizabeth Sanchez's name and mentions of Oregon in some of the communications. Do you want us to arrange some law enforcement protection in your area? We might be able to free up some FBI or DEA resources to help for a couple of weeks."

"Can I get back to you on that? I need to talk to Beth, uh, Ms. Sanchez, before we commit to anything."

"Sure. But don't take too long. I don't know how much longer the resources will be available, and we don't know how quickly these guys might make it to Oregon. They just crossed the border in a vehicle so, worst case, you have thirty-six to forty-eight hours before they will be in your area."

"What's local time for you, Preston?"

"Central daylight."

"Okay. It's almost 11:00 a.m. out here. I'll get back to you before 5:00 p.m. your time."

"Good luck, West. We'll be waiting to hear from you."

Drew hung up the phone and turned to face Beth.

Her face had lost its beautiful tan, the same look he'd seen when the rattler coiled near her face.

Drew wanted to erase it. To take it all away. But he couldn't. And his promise to protect her no matter what would likely cost him his life.

"They're coming for us, aren't they?" She forced the words out in a hoarse whisper.

He held her by the shoulders and peered into the brilliant, brown eyes, now wide and darting as if she was trying to see everything at once.

"I love you, Beth. Nobody hurts anyone I love. No matter what."

"What are you saying, Drew? This isn't three teenage punks. You can't take on Suarez and his men by yourself."

"It's more than Suarez and his men. He's teamed up with another cartel that does business in this area."

"They're planning another massacre. That's Suarez's MO. He did it to my town, to my family. Now he'll do it to this ranch, to you and your family, and to me."

"He can plan all he wants to. The best laid plans can fall apart with a little help from us ... or we can run. Either way, I need to tell Mom. She needs to get the kids out of here and move as many horses and foals as she can in the next thirty-six hours."

"Thirty-six hours? Is that all we've got?"

He pulled her into a tight embrace.

Beth didn't resist.

This is where she needed to be. Close to him. He would keep her with him until either he killed Suarez, or until Drew had no option but to sacrifice himself for her.

"Worst-case, we need to be ready in thirty-six hours. Preston said FBI Intelligence thinks they just crossed the border at Tijuana and that they were in a vehicle. Some other Del Rio men have already crossed the border and are in the US. If Suarez linked me to this ranch, I'm not that hard to find. Mom has a Facebook page for the ranch, and I'm sure some of her posts have mentioned me. We probably should have scrubbed her social media sites."

"Drew, when he attacked my town, Suarez surrounded it, completely destroyed the property of everyone he targeted, and he killed them all, family members, kids, even babies. Everyone but me. And here ... they will kill the horses too."

Drew stuck his head through kitchen doorway. "Mom, will you please come here for a minute."

"Mel, Coop, finish your desert at the kitchen table." She hurried into the dining room.

"We need to invoke our plan, but it may be worse than we thought."

"Drew, you're scaring me. What's happening?"

"We think a small army of cartel members is coming and could arrive here in as little as thirty-six hours. They will try to kill everyone, all the horses and probably burn the ranch."

His mom's hand went to her mouth. She plopped down onto the bench by the table.

"We need to move the horses. Call all the other ranchers and see how many trucks and pickups with trailers you can arrange and try to place all our horses somewhere, anywhere. Beth and I will keep Dusty and Sundown. We might need them. And, Mom, when you talk to the other ranchers, don't give them the details. Especially, don't mention drug cartels or they'll freak out. We don't have time to deal with that. Just say that some really bad dudes who don't like your son are coming and the horses are in danger too. Tell them we have to move them within twenty-four hours."

"They will ask a lot of questions, Drew."

"Act concerned and mention the urgency, but not the drug cartels"

He gave his mom the ranch phone. Drew pulled out his cell and sat on the bench. He looked up at Beth standing beside him. "Beth, how are you doing?"

"Not good. This is all my fault."

"Hey, I'm the one who did the personal damage to Suarez."

"Because of me."

"This isn't a time for arguing about blame. I need to call Agent Preston and tell him we could use some surveillance of our ranch. If an army is coming, the police won't be enough to stop them. But, if they're watching the area, at least law enforcement could warn us and maybe they could harass Suarez a bit to give us more time to get away. And maybe they can limit Suarez's movement."

Mattie hung up the phone and turned toward Drew. "I called Julia Bancroft at Crooked River Ranch. She said to bring Mel and Coop with me to her house."

Drew looked up at Beth.

She gave him a puzzled frown.

"Julia's husband, Steve, was a Ranger, Special Forces, a weapons sergeant. He'll keep them safe. But I don't think Suarez would find them there, anyway."

Mattie picked up the phone again. "I'm going to start calling all the ranchers. The kids and I will be safe. Just make sure you and Beth leave before the cartel can get here. And don't leave a trail for them to follow when you head for the cabin."

She looked at Beth, then back at Drew. Mattie shook her head. "I don't know what happened between you two, but fix it. *Now.* Life's too short for this nonsense. Besides, you don't want to go through what's coming with any distractions. You can't afford it. And you don't want to have any regrets."

His mom didn't say it, but Drew knew what she meant. You don't want to die with unresolved issues between you and the person you love. If that happens, you die alone ... or they do.

Chapter 17

Trucks, trucks and more trucks … with cars packed into all the spaces between them. That was why their big SUV wasn't moving.

Hector cursed the traffic, he cursed the dirty air of Los Angeles. But most of all, he cursed Mr. Drew West, because he was solely responsible for this excursion into the United States to right a wrong that had left Hector with a bad knee and a belly full of steroids that upset his stomach and spoiled his sleep.

Maybe tonight, when they arrived in Oregon, he would be thankful for the steroids. It might be a long, vengeful night.

His cell phone vibrated and played the Hawaii Five-0 theme. Ramon.

"Yes, Ramon."

"Hector, I thought you would never answer."

"I am traveling. Out of my usual area. It takes time even for the best technology to track me down and ring my cell. Do you have news? This late in our game, it must be good news, otherwise …"

"It *is* good news."

"Where are you, Ramon?"

"I am on a hill about a mile from the Way West Ranch looking through binoculars."

"Way West Ranch? What kind of idiots would name their rancho Way West? Do not answer that. It was a rhetorical question. Just tell me, what do you see through those binoculars?"

"Hector, how long have you been on those steroids? They seem to be making you—"

"That is not your concern. Now answer my question, Ramon, or I will ask a rhetorical question about your short lifespan."

"Yes, *El Capitan*. I can only see a couple of horses. But there are a lot of small barns with other horses probably for the brood mares."

"What about people? Who do you see?"

"No one. A truck drove away from the ranch when I arrived. But I don't see anyone outside. Maybe they went to the store or something."

"I am not hearing your good news, Ramon. Are you sure Drew West and Elizabeth Sanchez are there on West World Ranch?"

"Way West Ranch, *El Capitan*. Yes. They are here. Some young men in town saw them a day ago. They said West was like a madman, loco. They say he beat the—how do they say it here—the living crud—but Mr. West beat it out of these three young ruffians for insulting Señorita Sanchez."

"I will keep that in mind in case we need to make Mr. West angry. Keep watching the place, Ramon. I should be there tomorrow evening, after dark. I am bringing friends."

"But we do not have friends, Hector."

"As I told you earlier, we do now. The Tijuana cartel will help us, because I am returning the favor. This is their area. Central Oregon. If I cause trouble here, it affects their business. So I promised to make it up to them, and they are helping me."

"This is only a single ranch with one family. How many men will you bring?"

"I will have twenty of our own men and twenty from the Tijuana organization. We will have forty men to erase the ranch off the face of the earth and Señor West and Señorita

Sanchez with it. Stay and watch, Ramon. Report anything that is unusual."

"You are bringing a small army. That is probably overkill for this place."

"For my enemies, there is no such thing as overkill, Ramon. There is only kill until it is over. And it is over only when all the people, all their animals, and all their crops are killed and everything they own is completely destroyed. It is over only when the earth bears no record that they ever existed. *Comprende?*"

Chapter 18

11:00 a.m. the next day

"Drew, it's not even noon yet. We did it in twenty-four hours flat." They had done what Beth considered impossible. But people in horse country helped each other, as Drew had told her.

"Yeah. It was so good to see that last truck roll down the driveway a few minutes ago. Mom and the kids are safe. It's just you, me, Dusty and Sundown."

She couldn't help but smile. "My favorite foursome."

Drew's gaze met hers. "Even after day before yesterday?"

"That's just something we have to work on. Every couple has—" Beth stopped. A couple? She couldn't believe it. She was talking like she and Drew were engaged or already married.

He smiled. "Please continue, *mi amor.*"

"You're doing it again, Drew." It was the first time anyone had used that term to describe Beth Sanchez. And it resonated in her heart far more than when her father called her his *precioso tesoro.*

"Like you almost said. Every couple has some things to work on. Come on. Let's carry these packs to the barn and saddle up. We made it with twelve hours to spare, but let's get your favorite foursome on the trail early. We need to hide our tracks."

It only took Beth five or six minutes to saddle up Sundown and load her saddlebags. But what about their weapons? She glanced at Drew.

132

He trotted down the barn to the storage room and emerged a minute later with two rifles, scabbards and some boxes of ammunition.

So all I have to do is think about something and he gets it? That could lead to some interesting—

No, girl. It means you can't hide anything from that guy.

"Here's your rifle, Beth. Use the latigoes to hang the scabbard from the rings on your saddle. Don't put it so far forward that Sundown can't turn without her neck rubbing on it." He paused. "You do know how to shoot, don't you?"

If only Drew knew. Her father taught her well, but those were lessons that would be better forgotten. They raised memories that were better buried. The problem was the events she and Drew faced could resurrect every one of those horrid memories.

"I can shoot just fine, Drew. What are these? Lever action .30-30s?"

"Yeah. They're both loaded. And I'm bringing my Governor too. Actually, it's Mom's Governor, since that prosecutor in Pecos still has mine."

Five minutes later, Drew led the way on Dusty as they rode eastward down the driveway of the ranch. "Just in case someone is watching us, we're starting out headed east."

"The opposite direction from the cabin?"

"Yeah. Before we reach the road, we can circle back through the trees."

"Drew, the trees don't completely shield us if anyone is watching from one of the hills around us."

"They don't. But I have some more misdirection up my sleeve, Ms. Sanchez."

"I like Beth better."

Drew gave her a warm smile. "So we've set the clock back thirty-six hours?"

"You've got to start somewhere if you want to make things better."

"I'm not complaining. I've still got two of your ki—"

"Don't gloat or we'll go back to the Rio Grande and—"

"And your sexy swollen ankle?"

"Exactly."

Before they turned off the driveway and into the trees, Beth turned in her saddle and looked back at the ranch house and the barn. Would they be there when she and Drew returned? Would she return? If she did, would Drew be with her?

Things and people that were fast becoming part of Beth's life, a life she wanted more than anything Beth Sanchez had wanted in a long time, were anything but certainties. Hector Suarez could wipe it all away in minutes.

When one is battling evil of the worst sort, there are many uncertainties. But when the battle is with a drug cartel, there was one certainty. If you don't completely annihilate the evil, it will find a way to kill you.

Drew turned to the north for several minutes, until they reached a small creek that channeled irrigation runoff. They crossed it, emerging on rocky ground. Then Drew had them back their horses into the water, turn, and follow the creek for a quarter-mile. They left the creek on rocky ground, where they would leave few tracks.

"We're turning west now, toward the cabin. But, unless they have an expert tracker, I doubt they can follow our trail. They'll have to find some other way of locating us."

"Drew, how will we hide the horses at the cabin? There's no barn or shed."

"We have to leave the horses about a mile from the cabin. That's why we brought our big backpacks."

"Will they be okay?"

"There's good grass along an irrigation ditch where they can water. If we're discovered, and get into a foot race with anyone, we can try for the horses and use them to get away on the backroads and trails. This area is full of them."

"Do you have any idea how long we need to stay at the cabin, Drew?"

"I've got my cell. It's fully charged. I think we have to wait at the cabin until Agent Preston gives us the all clear signal."

"What if he doesn't?"

"We'll have to play that by ear. These guys won't stay forever, will they?"

"If they haven't found you, Drew, the cartel will stay. They will never stop unless all of us are dead. If they have to, they will stay until—how do you say it—until Hades freezes?"

* * *

Ramon stood at the pinnacle of the tallest hill he could find near the ranch. He held his cell to his ear and listened to Hector rant.

"We are passing through the capital of this overcrowded state that cannot seem to patch its roadways. One would think California is on the verge of bankruptcy. I may also be bankrupt if we hit any more bumps. They jar my teeth and I will not be able to pay the dentist to replace my fillings."

"I think the steroids are doing a number on you, Hector."

"Doing a number? Is that some vulgar American expression, Ramon? If it is—"

"No, Hector. I assure you it is not. Ees just that I remember being so full of prednisone that my face turned red like I had a fever. My head felt like a grenade after someone pulls the pin. I needed no sleep, and I would just as soon punch some hombre as to exchange words with him."

"So my detective understands that I am ready to explode. And I shall, Ramon, if I arrive at West World Ranch and—"

"Way West Ranch, *El Capitan.*"

"If I arrive at the rancho with the stupid name, and there is no Señor West or Señorita Sanchez, I will explode all over Ramon Vazquez. Where are they, Ramon? I must know before I arrive, or it will be an embarrassment to us. Luis Santana will begin to doubt us."

"Señor West and the girl rode away toward the east on two horses maybe two hours ago. They had heavy packs, and both horses had rifles on them. I think they plan to be gone for a while. I have not been able to spot them after they disappeared into the trees, but I have moved to a higher hill."

"You idiot! Someone alerted them. Was it you, Ramon? Did you say something to someone in the town?"

"No, *El Capitan.* I said nothing about Señor West or the ranch. I mostly listened."

"Who else is at the ranch? A big ranch must have vaqueros."

"I have seen no one. Just the pickup pulling a horse trailer. It was leaving. I told you when I called about nine o'clock this morning."

Had they moved their horses from this Westworld Ranch? Only if there was a leak. Suarez would find the leaker and, whether the leak was accidental or intentional, the man would die.

"Yes, you told me, Ramon. Now, I suggest you listen closely. I will arrive sometime around 11:00 p.m. It will be dark. If you have not found them by then, I will have no instructions for the men. I cannot burn the ranch and kill their animals unless I know where West and Sanchez are. We would be tipping our hand and could be forced to leave before we are finished. We would have spent a lot of money and taken risks all for nothing. Santana would not be happy. And Del Rio might end up fighting the Tijuana Cartel instead of punishing Señor West and the Sanchez girl."

"I will look for the horses, *El Capitan*. They will be easier to spot than people. And if I spot them, the Señor and Señorita will not be far away."

"You do that, Ramon. But you must find them before we arrive, or you will lose your usefulness to me. *Comprende?*"

Chapter 19

The ride to the cabin had been uneventful. It was 10:30 p.m. Over the past hour, darkness had enveloped the cabin and the thirty-six-hour deadline had elapsed.

The frequent lightning flashes to the east indicated that monsoon moisture had worked its way into the state from the desert Southwest.

Drew lit a single small oil lamp, then he stepped out of the cabin and studied the sky from the porch.

The thunderstorms were too far away to hear them. Probably near Prineville, seventy miles to the east of the cabin, and the ridge to the east blocked any direct view of them. But lightning flickered across the sky every few seconds, creating a strobe-light effect as it lit the towering clouds above.

It was an eerie and ominous display of power and light. Did it represent their lives? A flash of something promising snuffed out by the darkness?

A loud crack and a piercing light almost knocked Drew to the ground.

Beth ran out of the door and threw her arms around him. "Are you alright, Drew? That lightning was so close I thought ..."

"I'm okay." He returned her embrace. "But what's happening isn't good."

"You mean that thunderstorm coming in from the west?"

"Yeah. Let's go inside."

She pulled him through the door and kept his hand in hers once they were inside. "Are we safe this close to the top of the ridge?"

"We're safe in the cabin. There are higher things all around, pine trees, the ridge itself, all better grounding points than this cabin. But the weather could get violent tonight. Usually, the monsoon moisture from the Southwest doesn't make it to Oregon before late July or August. But it's here. And the marine air from the Pacific is undercutting it. It'll blow the lid off the tropopause."

"Are you a meteorologist or something? I thought you were a writer."

"I'm more like an 'or something'."

"I thought writers were always either writing or thinking about writing. But you've hardly talked about your writing, except mentioning that you needed ... uh, wanted me as your writing business manager."

"I was on a writing research trip to Texas, to Big Bend country. But I couldn't focus on my story, because I found a story that was more interesting."

"My story?"

"No. You."

"You got writer's block and you're blaming me?"

"No. I fell in love and I'm not blaming anybody."

Beth put her arms around him and laid her head on his chest. "But there is the reality of my story. It's a part of me, Drew, an awful, frightening part of me. And tonight, it feels like it's replaying."

"It's not. I'm not your father, Beth. I didn't try to drive a drug cartel out of its little fiefdom."

"No. You just ticked off the drug lord, which is exactly what Papa did. That was the catalyst that started everything that happened in Laguna."

"We've made our plan for dealing with Suarez. We've implemented it. It's a good plan, Beth."

A loud crack sounded, and it shook the cabin.

Beth's arms nearly choked him. "I have bad feelings about this night, Drew. I—I need you more than ever."

"I appreciate you telling me, INTJ girl." He smiled at her. She didn't reciprocate.

Someday soon she would be able to tell him that she loved him. But she did. Drew knew that, whether Beth used the words or not. And that was all that mattered.

Another bright flash of lightning lit the interior of the cabin. The boom came about ten seconds later.

"It's a couple of miles away and moving to the east. Probably dying."

They stood in the center of the living room, arms around each other, listening.

There was only silence. No distant lightning flashes. Nothing.

Drew pulled his arms from Beth and hooked an arm around her waist. "Something strange is happening out there. Let's open the door and listen."

Drew blew out the oil lamp.

They moved to the door.

He pulled it open, slowly, preventing it from creaking.

In the distance a noise came, one that didn't belong to the night.

"What was that sound?"

"I didn't hear anything." Beth pressed against his side.

"Let's listen."

It came louder this time. Somewhere, a horse had whinnied.

"Did you hear it?"

Beth nodded. Her head turned upward and her gaze locked on his face.

Two more loud neighs.

The whinnying became continuous.

The crack of two gunshots ripped through the stillness of the evening.

Beth's body froze against him. "The horses. It's Suarez."

The whinnying had stopped.

Suarez was here. If he had killed the horses, he would regret it.

A flash of lightning to the west lit Beth's face and revealed a tortured look that ripped at Drew's heart.

"He killed them and it's all my fault." Beth barely choked out the last word before her sobbing started.

"Not every bad thing that happens is your fault, Beth. Suarez chose to do what he did. But he didn't know that when he made that choice, he chose to die."

She swiped at her eyes. "No, Drew. I've cost you and your mom too much already. Please, don't do anything out of anger."

"I'm angry, but I'm not stupid. But Señor Suarez is. He just scheduled his funeral."

Beth gripped his wrists. "We will stay here, unless we're discovered, just like we planned."

"We can't just sit here and let him move in on us. If they found the horses, they will eventually find us. A good tracker can follow our trail as soon as it gets light. We need to go on the offensive, take the fight to them. If I can get Suarez, the fight is probably over."

"Listen to what you are saying. You want to take on an army and kill their general all by yourself. That's crazy. And what about me, Drew West. If you fail what happens to me?"

"Beth, if I stay here and let them come to us, I've failed you. The only possibility of success is to take out Suarez now. He won't be expecting it."

"I'm not going to stay here and listen to the shots that kill you. I—" Beth scampered to the wall and picked up the .30-30 she had leaned against it. "Are you going, Drew?"

"Yes. But you're not going with me."

"I'm not going with you, because you're not going either, even if I have to shoot you in the leg to stop you. You're not going!"

He stepped to his right, toward his gun leaning against the wall.

A telltale metallic sound said Beth had worked the lever and put a bullet in the firing chamber. "You're just like my father. Bent on getting yourself killed and others too. That's not being brave. It's just being a fool. Because he wouldn't back off, the cartel destroyed most of our town and they killed everyone who opposed them."

"Beth, if you're going to shoot me, you'd better shoot, because I'm going after Suarez. But if you shoot, he'll hear it. You'll be the one bringing him here."

She slammed her gun on the cabin floor, turned and pressed her face into the wall. Her body shook with each cry of her heart as the sobs came. From the sound of them, they would not stop anytime soon.

He couldn't stand this. Drew stepped outside and closed the door. Was he also closing the door on the best thing life had ever given him, Beth Sanchez?

* * *

Beth wiped her eyes and surveyed the room.

Drew had left, but he didn't take anything, so he wouldn't be gone long. He would come back, get his gun, and go out to face Suarez.

But if she left and told Drew it was over between them, he wouldn't have to protect her. It would make him safer no matter what he chose to do. And, with her gone, maybe he would choose not to go. Regardless, the biggest risk to Drew was to be saddled with Beth Sanchez.

She needed to tell him something if she left. She had to give him some reason. But she could never do that face-to-face.

Beth looked around the room for writing materials and found a few pens, pencils, and writing paper in the small desk. There were notes that looked like things Drew might have written while working on a novel.

Beth pulled out a sheet of blank paper and took one of the pens.

If she told Drew it was over between them, and that she was leaving, she could sneak out and maybe check on the horses on her way to Highway 126. As soon as it was light, she could catch a ride to Redmond, where she could call Sophia who would make travel arrangements for her to fly to Texas.

No. That wouldn't work. It might bring danger to Sophia.

The only solution was for Beth to simply disappear, like a self-imposed WITSEC program. Start a new life. Then there would be no trial in Pecos, with Drew there too. No troubled relationship with him. Just a new life and a new identity.

That wasn't what Beth wanted, but what she wanted in life always seemed to elude her.

She needed to hurry in case Drew returned. Her message needed to be brief and pointed. She quickly scrawled out her message.

Drew,

It would never work for us. I can see that and I'm sure you do too. I'm going away to a place where no one can find me, ever. Beth Sanchez no longer exists, so you should not look for her.

Goodbye, Drew

She read the note, then read it again. It sounded selfish. She hadn't even mentioned the danger they were in tonight with Suarez looking for them. And it was foolish to claim she could disappear and never be found. Would Drew buy any of it?

Beth had no choice but to try.

She put the note on the table and laid the pen on it, then she walked softly to the bedroom and slipped out the back door of the cabin. Hopefully, Drew was still at the other end of the building, on the front porch.

* * *

A bolt of lightning lit up the clouds above him and the area around him. Suarez looked toward the ridge to the west.

The lightning was both a blessing and a curse. It could reveal Drew West and the girl to him, but it might also give away his strategy and position.

Another flash lit the ridge.

Suarez mentally froze the brief video created by a flash of lightning illuminating that ridge. He had seen a figure moving toward the south, halfway down on this side of the ridge. That was the general direction of the horses he had shot at.

Maybe someone wanted to use the horses to try to escape. He could not let that happen.

"Manuel, take ten men and go back to where we saw the horses. I think someone is moving along the ridge to the west. I will take ten men and follow the ridge toward you. Whoever it is will be caught between us. I would bet money, a lot of money, that it is either Señorita Sanchez, Drew West, or both."

"We are on our way, *El Capitan*." Manuel motioned to his men and they scurried away to the east.

"Valdez, bring your men and follow me." He pointed at the ridge. "We run to the ridge, quietly. Then we move along it to the south, and we catch whoever is up there."

"Catch or kill?" Valdez said. "I do not want my men to make a mistake."

"Catch, unless they are going to kill you. Once we catch up to them, we surround them."

144

Three minutes later, Suarez's group had reached the base of the ridge and climbed part of the way up it.

Another thunderstorm bore down on them from the west. Lightning flashed on the far side of the ridge. But soon it would move to this side.

Right now, they needed to close on their quarry. Hector turned to Valdez and spoke softly, "I think they are only a hundred meters ahead, maybe two. We need to catch up to them now, before the lightning reveals us and spoils our night vision."

A buzzing came from behind Suarez. A yelp followed the buzz.

One of the men hurried to catch up with Valdez. "Arturo was bitten by a rattlesnake."

Suarez turned to the man. "Speak more softly, Gerardo. Did you kill the snake?"

Gerardo lowered his voice. "No, *El Capitan*. I do not think so. Arturo pinned its head to the ground with a stick."

"Arturo will not be any help tonight. He must stay here to rest and wait until we can help him back to the vehicles," Valdez said.

"But perhaps the snake will be of help. Secure it and bring it."

"Secure the snake? Are you sure, *El Capitan*?"

"I am always sure. Bring it. But hurry."

The pine and juniper trees were widely spaced now, and the undergrowth consisted of only a few bushes. Suarez's progress slowed as their cover grew sparse. So far, they had kept noise to a minimum.

A white flash stole his night vision and the loud, simultaneous crack stopped Suarez.

Lightning had struck the ridge top above them. A pine tree exploded into flames. It lit the area like a bright torch.

Movement ahead caught Suarez's attention. Denim shorts, long dark hair—it had to be Señorita Sanchez.

He pointed at her.

Valdez nodded.

Suarez motioned the men forward on his right and his left. "Stay with me Valdez," he whispered. "It is Señorita Sanchez. We wait here until the others have had time to flank her."

"*El Capitan*, I saw her," he whispered back. "And I also have seen pictures of Elizabeth Sanchez. It is a shame to kill a woman who looks like her."

"Then perhaps I should shame her instead of killing her. I could give her the great honor of belonging to the leader of the Del Rio Cartel."

"Or you could sell her, *El Capitan*."

"We shall see, Valdez. You sound as if you are ready to place a bid. Before we decide her fate, we must go claim Elizabeth Alicia Sanchez, daughter and only living child of that foolish *hombre*, Rafael Sanchez."

* * *

Beth needed to hurry. Put as much distance between her and the cabin as she could before the lightning started again and lit the whole area, including her.

She could not let Drew find her, or he would stop her from going. Her resolve would crumble with one look at the pain in his eyes.

Had Beth just admitted that she was running from Drew against her own will? Her logic seemed to say that. But she had to run, because Beth was weak. Beth Sanchez couldn't stand up for herself, couldn't do what was right. If she could, she would have died eight years ago.

A crunching noise came from her left, below Beth on the side of the ridge.

Another sound, a crack, came from her right, somewhere above her.

Maybe it was deer moving toward the water where they had left the horses. But the electricity shooting tingling sensations up her back suggested otherwise.

She crouched beside a large bush and listened.

The sound below her had now moved in front of her and more sounds came from behind and above her. Either it was deer, or Beth Sanchez was surrounded.

Heavy boots clomped on the ground all around her.

She curled into a ball, hid under the bush, and tried to control her heavy breathing.

I wish Drew was here.

Then why did you dump him with that nutty note?

She was a fool. Beth usually thought things through, thoroughly. Her desperate action, based only on her emotions, could cost her everything.

A flashlight beam flooded the area with light.

The beam moved her way.

Now, it lit her body.

"Me estás tomando el pelo?" It was Suarez's gravelly voice, filled with surprise. "No, you aren't kidding me."

She didn't want to appear as a cowering fool. Beth stood and looked his way, but could only see the bright, blinding light.

"Valdez, bind her hands behind her back." Suarez's voice.

Beth kicked at the shadowy figure that approached her. She threw an elbow at another person, but rough hands pushed her face down to the ground and held her there.

Her stomach roiled at the stench of unwashed bodies. She wanted to turn and vomit her disgust on them. Show them how much she detested these vile men. But she couldn't move.

In a few seconds, her wrists were tied, and the nylon bands cut into her skin with each attempt to break free from them.

"Señorita Sanchez ..." It was the raspy voice of Suarez. "Before you entertain me, you should tell me where your lover, Drew West is hiding. If you tell me now, it could spare you much ... discomfort. But you will tell me, regardless."

Though she wanted to, Beth forced herself not to reply.

"Maybe I should spoil *tu hermoso rostro*. Would that help your memory?"

Mar her face? He was capable of a lot more than that, but Beth didn't want to give in if he was only bluffing at this point. She wouldn't make it easy for them to catch Drew.

"I don't know where he is. I had an argument with him and ran away. I was still running when you found me."

"And you are a liar, Señorita."

"A liar? You can call me anything you want. It does not change the truth."

"Call you anything? Very well, perhaps I will call you mine ... and let you live, if you tell me where Señor West is."

Though she feared Suarez, his taunting threats brought heat to the back of her neck—two-hundred-twelve-degree heat. "I told you I don't know. But I wouldn't tell you even if I did."

"Now we are getting to the truth, are we not?"

She pulled her legs under her, rose to her knees, and glared up a Suarez. "*You* tell *me*, coward who kills children."

"Coward?" His face contorted into an ugly caricature of itself. "No! Suarez kills his *enemies*! Big ones, little ones, all my enemies. *Comprende*?"

"You kill children. That I could never *comprende*."

"Then maybe you will understand this. You will not tell me where Señor West is, so I will persuade him to come to us. Do you know how I do this, Señorita?"

"It sounds like a magician's trick. Maybe Hector Houdini should surprise me."

His face morphed to an uglier version of itself.

She shouldn't have said that.

Suarez turned to the man behind him. "Tell Gerardo to bring the stick."

Stick? Were they going to beat her?

Somehow Suarez was going to use her to lure Drew. She was a fool to think that Drew might be safe if she were out of the picture. Suarez was obsessed with killing Drew. Probably because of what Drew had done to him at Santa Elena Canyon, including shooting his little brother.

Suarez would lure Drew, kill him slowly and painfully, then turn his attention to Beth. Suarez's words replayed in her mind.

Perhaps I will call you mine ... and let you live.

It would be better if Elizabeth Sanchez were dead than to suffer the horror-filled life and depravity Suarez had in mind. Maybe she could force him to kill her quickly. At first opportunity, she could fight him so savagely—biting, kicking, clawing at him, screaming insults—that he would have to kill her.

But the truth was, Beth was too much of a coward to attack Suarez. Then there was the greatest truth of all ... Suarez should have already killed her ... eight years ago. Both Drew and Beth would be far better off if he had.

Chapter 20

Drew ignored the lightning and the thunderstorms which had brought no rain. He paced the ground in front of the cabin and tried to face the truth, the truth that he wasn't worthy of a woman like Beth Sanchez.

Beth was a good and beautiful woman, a survivor in a world filled with evil and violence.

Somehow, Drew must stop the violence of Hector Suarez. But the truth, once again, slammed him to the ground to grovel in the low place reserved for the inadequate people of the world, those who couldn't measure up.

And what would happen if Drew went after Suarez and ended up getting Beth hurt or killed? The pain would make his life unbearable.

Maybe he could checkout of life. He could find Suarez, walk into his camp, and die while killing the man. But there was no guarantee Drew could accomplish that, even if he was willing to die to kill that snake, Suarez.

Drew had developed considerable skill with weapons. He had honed his martial arts skills to near perfection. But none of that was enough to insure his success.

In the distance, a cry sounded. It had come from the west, somewhere near the base of the ridge. The cry rose above the low rumble of the thunderstorms. Was it the scream of a woman? Or was it a bobcat?

Beth? It couldn't be her.

His heart hammered in his chest.

Drew slung open the front door and ran into the cabin.

Beth wasn't there.

His eyes focused on a pad of paper and a pen on the table. They hadn't been there earlier.

Hands shaking and fearing the worst, he walked to the table. A short note had been scrawled on the paper.

He read the note. It punched all the air from his lungs and all the life from his heart.

Beth had preferred risking Suarez to escape from Drew. How could her contempt for him be so strong that she preferred falling into the hands of Suarez? And how could disdain grow so rapidly in a heart he believed he had won?

Only one answer came.

You are a failure, Drew. Inadequate for any worthy task or goal. There is no reason for your existence.

Where had those words come from? Regardless, they seemed to summarize what Drew's grandfather had said when Drew failed to protect his sister.

He heard the sound again, so loud it came through the cabin walls.

A woman screaming.

"Drew ..." Now, it was his grandfather's voice. "I bought you that rifle because I thought you were a man. But you wouldn't even use it to protect your sister. You don't have it in you to be a man. Not a man in the West family."

The scream came again, ear-piercing, heart-piercing, but intelligible.

"Help me!"

He snatched his rifle from where it stood, shoved his handgun in his belt, ran out the door, and turned toward the direction of the screaming.

In the distance, lights flickered and danced among the trees near the base of the ridge about a half mile away.

Was it a trap? Probably. That no longer mattered. The woman he loved, but didn't deserve, was being tortured by a demon-driven drug lord, a man Drew would kill, even if it was the last act of a desperate man.

Using the flashes of lightning when they came, relying on pure luck when they didn't, Drew ran recklessly toward the screams. Since he was running downhill, he approached the lights and commotion in a couple of minutes.

But was he in time?

He slowed and crept from tree to tree, trying to gain a position that gave him a view of Suarez and his men.

A shadowy figure leaped at him from behind a bush.

Drew swung his rifle with all his strength.

It cracked on the man's skull and drove his head into the ground.

Drew knelt and looked at the gash on the man's head and then studied his chest. He wasn't breathing.

Drew had killed a sentry. Did that mean this side of Suarez's camp was no longer guarded? Maybe.

Drew moved to another tree, closer to Suarez, then jerked to a stop when he saw Beth.

Twenty or thirty men stood around her. Several held flashlights on her.

Suarez had bound her hands then tethered her to a tree on a short length of rope that allowed her to move two or three feet from side to side.

A short, stocky man shoved a stick at her.

Beth screamed.

A rattlesnake buzzed loudly.

Drew now understood both the method of torture and the reason for it. Suarez wanted Drew.

Please, God, help me. Beth doesn't deserve this.

Drew moved closer and stood behind another tree. He could go no further without being seen. He checked both guns and stood.

Drew, I did not make you inferior, but you must find

152

your adequacy in me.

Had he thought those words or heard them? Or, had he recalled them from memory, from a time in the distant past?

I am your strength and your shield. Without me you can accomplish nothing. Some trust in weapons of warfare, but you must trust in me, the Lord your God.

Bits of scripture he had memorized as a child now joined together in a meaningful context. The truth about his past became clear. For Drew, it had been a matter of misplaced trust. Seventeen years of misplaced trust, nearly two decades of trusting his fighting ability more than trusting the Lord his God.

I am the One who goes before you to fight against your enemies to give you the victory.

Outnumbered thirty or forty to one, Drew couldn't do this on his own. But he must do it for Beth. He would do what he could, even give his life, but God would have to intervene for this to turn out right. God would have to give Drew the victory.

Drew studied the position of each man.

Thirty men stood around Beth. Others probably guarded the area.

He rehearsed his movements, where he would strike, where he would kick, and where he would shoot. He might kill fifteen or twenty before they got him. Regardless, Suarez would be the first to die.

He told Beth that Suarez had scheduled his funeral. And Drew would make good on his promise.

Before he charged Suarez's camp, Drew prayed that his attack would be enough to spare Beth's life. That would have to be his victory. It was the best outcome Drew could hope for in an almost hopeless situation.

* * *

The lightning flashed and again the snake went berserk. With its head tied to the stick, it coiled and struck, sending its tail shooting out behind it, but its head remained stationary on the stick.

This allowed the man holding the stick to shove it near Beth's face, where she could see the fangs open and protrude and the venom drip from them after each attempted strike.

Beth was through screaming because of the snake. Her voice was nearly gone anyway.

She hadn't tried to remain stoic, hadn't tried to stifle her screams. If she hadn't screamed, Suarez would have resorted to something even worse. Eventually, she would scream and Drew would come.

But something had just changed in the group of men enjoying her torture. She listened.

The subject of their talk had changed from the snake to Beth.

"*El Capitan*, instead of killing her, why don't you auction her off. I would pay fifty thousand dollars for a woman like her."

"Maybe I should keep her," Suarez said. He turned toward her. "Señorita Sanchez, shall I give you the honor of belonging to the CEO of the Del Rio Cartel? He is a wealthy man."

"I will tell you what you can do with your offer, Hector."

"Those are not the words that will spare your life, Ms. Sanchez."

Spare her life? It would be better to die of a snake bite to her neck than to belong to Suarez. Maybe the next time they shoved the snake at her, she would move toward it instead of away.

But she deserved all of this. She had lied to her mother that night, then went with her friends to a place that her parents disapproved of. Beth was away from home, in another town, disobeying her parents, when they were brutally killed by Suarez.

She was getting what she should have gotten eight years ago. At least now the guilt would end ... either quickly or slowly.

I know, God, this is what I deserve. But please make them kill me quickly.

She looked up at Suarez.

The twisted smile on his face told her quick was the last thing on his mind.

* * *

Drew had heard enough of the men yelling vile insults at Beth. He had heard enough of her screaming, and he'd seen and heard enough from that blasted rattlesnake.

Drew checked his rifle and handgun one more time.

At least he had the element of surprise. Suarez wouldn't believe Drew could be so foolhardy as to attack a whole army by himself. But Suarez's mistaken belief would cost him his life in about thirty seconds.

Drew had asked for help but had seen nothing yet.

Maybe this was one of those times when you had to stick your foot in the Jordan before anything happened.

All the men seemed to be looking at Beth.

Time to put my foot in the water.

He stepped out from behind the tree and took a step toward Suarez.

A hand curled around his face, clamping over his mouth. It yanked him back to the tree.

Fingers like vice grips clamped onto his gun hand.

"Easy, Drew. It's Steve. Steve Bancroft."

"But how did—"

"Your mom and the kids are safe. We thought you might need me more than they did.'

"They've got Beth and—"

"I know. Now here's what we're going to do."

Chapter 21

Even with Steve helping Drew, the odds were at least forty to two against them. But Steve was ex-military, an Army Ranger who was the weapons specialist for his team. And his presence brought a mixture of hope and anxiety while sending adrenaline coursing through Drew's body.

Steve unslung his pack and opened it. "This is stuff left from the martial law and near civil war we had eight years ago." He pulled out two grenades.

'These are M84 flashbang grenades." He pointed through the tree branches to the cluster of men around Beth. "By my count, there are thirty men surrounding Beth. If we hit them with these two grenades, simultaneously, we'll incapacitate about half and temporarily stun the rest. It should buy us enough time for you to run in and carry her out. Anybody who's not stunned, or comes in from guarding the perimeter, I'll take out with my M4."

This could actually work. Drew's hope surged as Steve continued his explanation of their plan.

"After we flashbang them, my job is to shoot anybody who looks like they can handle a gun. Your job is to go in, cut Beth's ties, and carry her back to this spot as fast as is humanly possible. Got a knife?"

Drew nodded. "And I can do that in about fifteen to twenty seconds."

"I can hold them off that long. It's no problem, unless somebody close to Beth isn't impacted much by the grenades."

"Is that possible?"

"Yes, but not likely. And it's also why the grenades need to land as close to Beth as we dare."

"How close is that?"

"Six to ten feet. But no closer."

Drew picked up one of the grenades and bounced it in his hand. "Do you want me to throw one of these? We could deliver them simultaneously."

"How's your arm?"

"I pitched baseball in high school. Had good control."

Steve dipped his head. "You take the left side of the group and I'll take the right side. Some people will be blinded, some deafened and dizzy, and a few knocked out. I'm guessing Beth will be nearly knocked out. If we're lucky, she'll be looking the other way or will have bodies between her and the flash. Then she'll recover more quickly. But there is one danger we can't overlook."

"Could this kill Beth?"

"No. Not likely. These things are hot when they ignite, so don't hit Beth. But we could start a forest fire."

"The lightning's been threatening to do that all evening. It's a risk worth taking."

"Agreed. When you get back here with Beth, we reassess to see if we need to wait a minute or so for her to gain her senses and balance enough to run. If she can't run, you'll have to carry her out of here."

"Which way are we going? Up the ridge?"

"Yes. We'll retreat toward the ridge behind us and continue westward until we lose them. I've got more to tell you, but you need to get her out of there now. That group around her is working itself into a frenzy. Here's your grenade. Pull the pin on three, by my count, and throw it. Then cover your eyes and ears until both grenades have detonated. And pitcher ... we can't afford a balk. From the time you start, throw the ball in one continuous motion."

"Got it." Drew pulled out his pocketknife and palmed it in his left hand.

"Don't dilly dally after we move out into the open."

They stepped out from behind the tree.

"Drew, here we go. One ... two ... three."

Drew's strategy was to throw a strike. He threw a fastball at a man who stood six feet to the left of Beth. The grenade hit him in the back.

Drew covered up. But even at this distance, the shock wave slammed his head like a rubber mallet. Then Drew sprinted toward the goal, Beth Sanchez.

Some men lay on the ground. Others staggered around like they couldn't see. Many covered their ears and slumped over like they were in pain.

Drew wove between them like a running back shredding a bad defensive secondary.

The staccato cracking of Steve's M4 began with several short bursts.

A gun fired somewhere in the trees.

Steve's rifle shot a long burst.

The return fire ended.

The rattlesnake stick bounced around among the men as the snake struck, repeatedly, but ineffectively.

Drew jumped over the snake and reached Beth.

She sat on the ground at the base of the tree where they had tethered her.

He slid behind her and cut the tether, then the ties, and scooped her up in his arms.

"Drew ..."

That's all she said, but it was enough for now. It sent him sprinting in Steve's direction as gunfire erupted all around him.

He scampered past Steve and circled behind the tree for protection.

Steve shot a long burst that must have emptied his magazine.

It temporarily silenced the cartel's guns.

Steve joined Beth and Drew behind the big tree.

"I'm sorry, Drew. I lied. Please forgive me ... stupid ... so stupid." Beth's first coherent words after the grenades.

"It's okay, Beth. There won't be any more arguments like that, ever."

Steve shoved a magazine into his M4 and laid a hand on Drew's shoulder. "You two can take care of the relational stuff later. We need to get out of here. They're about to start shooting again. We've got them scared, so they'll shoot at anything that moves."

Steve studied Beth for a couple of seconds, then he nodded. "Sorry we had to flash bang you."

"You had to what? It doesn't sound decent ... whatever it means."

"Just so you know, I had to flash bang my wife, Julia, once. But that was before we were married. Back when the whole country came unglued."

Beth sat up in Drew's arms. He lowered her to the ground.

"What exactly did you do to me? I'm almost afraid to ask."

"We used a concussion grenade to stun you and all the men around you." Steve flashed a grin. "Suarez was on my side, so I made sure my grenade landed beside him. He won't hear well for the rest of the evening. Maybe for the rest of his life. The whole camp is in chaos. But we've got to get out of here before he recovers and starts giving orders to his men."

Drew set Beth on the ground and clamped his hands on her waist to steady her. "Can you stand and walk?"

"Which one? I don't know if I can do both at the same time."

"She's still a little punchy," Steve said. "Give her about twenty seconds, and I'll bet she can run with a little assistance."

Drew hooked her waist and pulled her against his side. "Let's try a few steps."

She took off running, pulling Drew with her.

"We're ready, Steve."

Steve retreated with them. "Great. Here's your rifle. You two run up the hill and head west. I'm going to be the decoy. I'll get them to follow me, so you can get away."

Steve had saved their lives. He had no stake in this, and Drew couldn't put him in further danger. "No, Steve. Don't sacrifice yourself."

"I said decoy, not sacrifice. Big difference."

Drew wasn't convinced. He'd heard stories about special forces warfighters who felt driven to take chances, obligated to risk their lives. Others got thrills from intense action, firefights, and camouflaging themselves to sneak up on the enemy and attack them.

"Drew, I did this for a living. These cartel guys aren't well-trained. Besides, if the temperature here was equal to their IQs, you'd have to button up your jacket or freeze. You two go west. You know the area, Drew. Lose these losers. I'll be fine."

"Steve, I ..." He couldn't find the words to convey what he felt for Steve. "I think ... I think God sent you after I demanded that He—"

"I know. Guys in combat do a lot of demanding and a little begging. He understands. Maybe God did send me, but the cartel goons probably think it was the devil." Steve chuckled.

"Beth and I will be okay, thanks to you. Play it safe, Steve. Don't take any chances."

Drew hooked his right arm around Beth's waist and, with his rifle in his left hand, started the long run up the ridge.

They had freed Beth from the cartel goons. She was with him. But a lot had happened in the past hour. If they both survived the night, would their relationship ever be the same?

Chapter 22

Halfway up the ridge, Drew stopped behind a bushy juniper tree. He put a hand to his brow and scanned the sky. "Something's happening with the thunderstorm situation. Whatever it is, it's not good."

The lightning had become more frequent. Each flash revealed numerous towering thunderstorm cells.

Beth and Drew couldn't move without lightning revealing them to anyone scanning the ridge.

On the positive side, Steve could allow Suarez to see him, making it easier to lead the cartel gunmen away.

Beth leaned over his shoulder and pointed to the plateau below them. "Suarez and his men are following Steve. From the bouncing flashlights, there are twenty or thirty of them."

"After Steve's shooting, that's probably all that are alive." He nudged Beth up the hill. "We need to get over the ridge and out of sight while they're still chasing Steve."

Beth pulled his hand from her waist. "I'm okay now. Race you to the top."

Drew ran hard while trying to watch Beth ahead of him and the cartel in the area below. He stumbled over a small windfall.

If he didn't pay more attention to his feet, he could turn an ankle. That could get them killed.

When he and Beth crossed the ridgeline, a prolonged series of in-cloud lightning flashes lit the ridge around them.

Before he lost sight of the Suarez's men below, Drew looked back toward them.

Their flashlights had reversed direction and now moved up the ridge toward Beth and him.

Drew stopped to verify his conclusion.

Beth stopped too and looked at him, concern showing on her face with each bolt of lightning.

"Yeah. They saw us, Beth. We've got a big lead, so let's head for Steelhead Falls."

Thirty minutes later, Beth and Drew stood, breathing heavily, on the flat rock protruding into the Deschutes River below the falls.

The tiny droplets of water flung into the air by the waterfall cooled the skin on Drew's arms and legs. It was refreshing, but their intermission would be a short one.

The question was, did they have time to talk? They needed to. That cryptic note needed to be discussed and disposed of.

He looked down into Beth's eyes. It wasn't the right time for discussing their issues. But it was impossible to ban them from his consciousness. They interrupted his thinking like the lightning did his vision. "Beth, have you seen any lights since we crossed the ridge?"

"No. Only a lot of lightning. But we need to leave, now." Another flash revealed the frown and Beth's searching eyes, searching his for resolution. "You're thinking about the note. I can tell."

"Yeah. But—"

"Drew, you've got to realize I wasn't saying what I wanted, only what I thought I had to say to save your life, but ..."

"But it wouldn't have worked, would it?"

"No. But I was desperate. I think God knew that, so He gave me something better. An Army Ranger and the man that I—"

"Beth. Up the trail. Are those flashlights?"

Her head turned toward the trail. "Well, they aren't fireflies."

"How did they know to come this way after they crossed the ridge?"

"Maybe Suarez is part bloodhound. Or part devil. So what do we do now? They will be here in another ten minutes."

"I think we can lose them here."

"We can't lose anyone standing here in the open. What do you mean, Drew?"

"I meant to tell you when we were here earlier, but I got distracted by a pretty señorita. There's a cave at water level on the other side. It has two openings about twenty feet apart. Can you dive? The water's deep enough here. I've done it since I was a kid."

"I can dive."

"I'll go, then you after me. Swim straight across and I'll help you into the cave."

"Isn't that putting all of our eggs into one basket? If they spotted us in the cave, we'd be trapped."

"No. We can slide out the small opening while their lights are on the other one. The small opening is at water level. I don't think they will see it." He paused. "How far can you swim underwater?"

"I can stay under for almost a minute."

"That should work. If we have to escape underwater, we'll swim downstream. You've got to push it to your limits. Come up for a breath and go under again. When we come back up, we'll be almost a hundred yards downstream. There's cover. We can get out unseen and head for that pine tree canyon."

"What about your rifle, Drew?"

"It's not much use against AK-47s. I'll hide my .30-30 and just keep the Governor."

"Will it be okay after being in the river?"

"Yeah. Thanks to modern ammo."

Drew hid his rifle under a ledge below the large, flat rock they stood on. He turned, facing the water at the edge of the rock. "Time to take a dip. I'll surface and wait for you. There's a bit of a current, so we don't want to dilly dally, or we'll end up swimming upstream to reach the cave. That might allow them to get here in time to spot us. When you get out, try to climb out on the left side of the cave opening, where the grass grows over the rocks. We don't want them to see our wet path. Ready?"

Her shadowy head nodded.

Drew took a step to the edge of the rock and launched his body into the darkness ahead of them. It wasn't a perfect dive, but the noise of the falls would cover his splash.

He surfaced and treaded water.

Drew didn't hear Beth hit the water. Where was she? More importantly, where were Suarez and his men?

The flashing lights on the trail were only two- or three-hundred yards away. They could be here in a couple of minutes.

Beth bobbed up beside him. They almost bumped heads.

"Follow me, Beth. We need to hurry." Drew dogpaddled the ten yards to the rocky shore at the base of the cliff that housed the cave.

When he felt the bank, he pulled his body across the grassy area and waited.

Beth was only a couple of seconds behind.

He took her hands and pulled her out of the water. "Hurry. Into the cave, then we'll move to our right. It's about twenty feet to the other opening."

The cave was smaller than Drew remembered. His adult body had to squeeze through the rocks at the midway point, but he made it to the other opening.

Once again, Beth followed on his heels.

Drew looked back to where they had entered.

A bright beam lit the other opening. The beam focused on the wet rocks that gave away their entry into the cave.

How were Suarez and his men able to follow Beth and Drew at night despite his efforts to lose them? Maybe it was the lightning. If it didn't stop soon, the thunderstorms might end up killing Beth and him.

Suarez was still inspecting the other cave opening. Time to get out of the cave and into the water.

"*Quién puede nadar?*" One man pointed down from the rock where he stood to the water.

"*No. Ellos estan atrapados. Esperaremos.*" It sounded like Suarez's voice.

"What are they saying?"

"One man is asking if someone can swim across, but Suarez says to wait, because we're trapped."

He tugged on Beth's hand. "Let's go before we *are* trapped. The water's deep. We can just slide in and go under. Stay to the left side of the river. About a hundred yards downstream there's a slight bend in the river and there's cover. We can get out behind the trees. They won't be able to see us. Remember, go as far as you can before you come up for air. Push it until you can't stand it one second longer. When you do come up, stay low. Only let your face out of the water. I'll be waiting to swim the second leg with you."

"How will I find you?"

"You won't have to. I'll find you."

She squeezed his hand and Drew lowered himself into the chilling water.

He sucked in a breath, completely filling his lungs, and pushed his body under.

Drew had forgotten how cold this river's water feels when swimming below its surface. The glacier-fed water of the Deschutes stings a person's eyes, freezes their forehead, and produces other discomforts that make a person want to surface.

Was Beth up to this? As Drew frog kicked underwater, he prayed she was. He prayed *he* was. And he prayed that there would be no lights shining on their heads when they surfaced for air.

When his lungs screamed for air, Drew didn't give in. He counted slowly to ten and then let his face break the water's surface. He sucked hard two or three times then pushed against the water with his hands and swiveled to look up the river.

Beth's head broke the surface about five yards upriver from him. She had done well. She had pointed her feet upstream and was floating down the river with only her face exposed. A smart move. Maximizing breathing time, minimizing her exposure.

He waited for her to catch up with him.

Lights now danced on the water all around the falls. One of them moved slowly down the river, exploring both sides.

Drew spun around to look downriver.

The small point hosting a tree had a small boulder beside it. It was too dark to tell for sure, but it looked like the point would keep them sheltered from prying eyes. The rock would stop bullets if they were spotted.

Beth caught him and took his hand.

"Beth, they're starting to look downriver. We need to make it to the point that's about thirty yards downstr—"

A bright flash of lightning lit the entire river valley around them. The sharp crack came only a second behind the flash.

A cacophony of voices rose in volume from the group by the falls. The dreaded tat-tat-tat sounded, and columns of water exploded into the air beside Beth.

They needed the protection of the water.

"Go deep and go all the way." Drew dove and pulled her down with him.

Beth's hand slipped from his and she shot ahead of him. Her power as a swimmer surprised him. Maybe they could make it to the bend without surfacing and becoming targets.

Another flash of lightning lit the water. It outlined Beth as she swam underwater, ahead and slightly above him.

She needed to be deeper to—no. The rounds fired at them were hitting the water at an acute angle. That would provide the required eight feet of water to slow the bullets to a harmless speed.

The zip, zip of bullets striking the water above them punctuated the underwater silence. The shots continued for a few seconds then stopped.

Did that mean Suarez thought he'd hit them? If Drew and Beth remained out of sight after surfacing at the point, maybe Suarez would think he'd killed them. If he started looking for their dead bodies, Beth and Drew could regain their big lead, provided the lightning didn't give them away as they climbed out of the small river valley.

Drew focused on the shoreline, hoping another flash of lightning might show him Suarez's position.

In a few seconds, a flash and a near simultaneous boom sent pain through his ears though he was underwater. But the lightning had shown Drew a rock directly beside him.

He reached up where Beth's body had been and felt the smooth skin of her leg. He reached again. His hand found an ankle. He pulled it toward shore.

Beth made the course correction.

They were going to make the sheltered point.

Drew pulled hard on the water and broke the surface beside the rock.

The burping of an AK-47 accompanied by flashes of light came from up river. But this time, it came from well below the falls.

Suarez must have seen the ripples in the smooth water. He hadn't given up, and he was coming downstream, following them.

He and Beth needed to get out of the water and climb out of the river valley before they were spotted again.

Beth glided into the bank beside him. They were safe behind the rock but only until Suarez came another fifty yards downstream.

They didn't have time to wait for Beth to catch her breath. "We need to make a run for it, now. Take my hand and try to keep up."

With wet clothes and soggy shoes, Drew seemed twenty pounds overweight as he sought a path up the west side of the Deschutes River canyon in the darkness.

The bank wasn't as steep here and, once they crossed the ridge above them, they would be near the mouth of the pine tree canyon. But they needed the lightning to cooperate, or they might never make it out of the river canyon alive.

Lightning struck the ridge on the east side of the river. The light revealed a small path ahead of them. "Head for the deer trail on our left. We'll run the trail to the top."

"And pray we're behind a tree when the lightning flashes," Beth said.

If Suarez spotted them scurrying up the side of the small canyon, he and Beth would be easy targets for twenty-five men all carrying AK-47s. Firing about eight rounds a second, that was what ... two-hundred bullets a second coming at them.

Why had he even made that calculation? They would need something more than just luck to get out of the river valley without being hit.

Drew prayed for help to get Beth safely over the next ridge. Maybe that was why he'd made that crazy calculation. It had reminded him of their need and that they weren't in this drama alone. Regardless, it was time to make their run.

Drew tugged on Beth's arm and they sprinted along the deer trail climbing the slope. He pulled her to a stop behind the first tree they reached.

A flash of lightning turned the river valley brighter than the noonday sun.

"We can't let them catch us in the open when it flashes like that."

Beth nodded. "There's no excuse for what I did, but I trust you Drew. I always have."

With all that was happening, Beth's mind was obviously on her note and her leaving.

Somehow, he had grown so engrossed with protecting her, that he'd forgotten the note. Drew wanted to finish discussing that topic, to remove whatever barriers remained between him and the only woman he had ever loved. But this wasn't the time.

Regardless, her words lifted Drew up. But at the same time, they weighed him down with the responsibility of keeping Beth alive.

"Beth, let's go again. But if we do get caught in the open when the lightning flashes, we'll reverse direction and run back to the last tree we passed."

"Got it. Don't let them use the lightning to their advantage."

Drew nodded then pulled her back onto the deer trail. They ran as fast as they dared in the darkness and, in four or five seconds, reached a large juniper. When they slipped behind it, in-cloud lightning, directly above them, lit the river valley.

"Good timing, Drew." She squeezed his hand.

"As if I had anything to do with that."

"Without His help, we wouldn't have made it this far."

Drew nodded again, but what had he just acknowledged?

In situations like this, with serious danger and lives on the line, Drew never knew where his responsibility ended and God's began. Maybe the two were merged such that Drew didn't have to worry about separate responsibilities. Maybe he needed to do his best and leave supplying whatever was lacking to God.

Leaving anything to someone else wasn't something Drew West was good at. He was better at pounding opponents into submission than submitting his will to the One who gave Drew his fighting ability.

Beth poked his shoulder. "Time to go."

"Yeah." He needed to keep his mind in the game. It seemed like the fourth quarter with Beth and Drew ahead by one point. They were ahead, but if they fell behind, it was game over.

Before they ran from behind the tree, a cloud-to-ground bolt of lightning struck the ridge top above them. In the flicker of light, Drew could see the distance that remained. They had seventy-five yards left with two trees for cover and no obstacles on the trail.

He tugged on Beth's hand.

They reached the next tree, and there had been no more lightning, so Drew continued their run up the trail.

Another in-cloud flash lit Beth and Drew with its white light. The next tree stood only ten yards ahead. Instead of reversing direction as they had planned, Drew broke into an all-out sprint up the hill.

The staccato burping of multiple automatic weapons echoed through the canyon.

Drew kept running, pulling Beth.

Bullets kicked up dust around them.

Dirt stung his bare legs.

He swung Beth, by the hand, around his body until she was ahead of him. Maybe Drew's body could stop the bullets before they reached Beth.

They slid to a stop at the next tree.

Drew pushed Beth behind its thick trunk.

Pain!

A stinging in his upper left arm quickly morphed to spasming muscles. His triceps turned as hard as a rock.

Something tickled the skin on his arm. The sensation ran down to his wrist.

Drew touched his wrist with his right hand. Warm, sticky … blood.

The shooting stopped.

He hid behind the tree with Beth and waited for the pain to subside.

Should he tell her he was hit? No. He needed to rest here and see how bad it was. The blood had been *trickling* down his arm, not flowing. Maybe he'd just been nicked.

"What are you doing." Beth reached for his arm, before he could react.

She pulled her hand back after touching his forearm. "You're bleeding. Drew, you need to talk to me. Tell me what's happening."

"You're a fine one to be making that point."

Beth's face tilted down toward the ground. Her shoulders slumped.

"I'm sorry, Beth. Getting hit can make a guy say crazy things."

She looked up. "How bad is it?"

"They nicked my upper arm. I think it's only a deep scratch."

"How deep?"

"I can't tell. It's too dark."

"Turn your arm my way." Beth gripped his shoulders and turned him.

Lightning flashed in the cloud above them and thunder rumbled for several seconds. It lit his wound enough for her to get a glimpse.

"I need to bandage it."

He couldn't see the wound on the back of his arm. "How bad is it, Beth?"

"It needs more than a Band-Aid."

"We had a first aid kit at the cabin. If we hadn't—"

"Drew, let's not go there. Not now. Give me your knife."

"My knife? Can I trust you with it?"

"What do you think?"

He imagined her enigmatic smile, one that would complement her enigmatic words.

Drew blew out a breath. Too bad he couldn't also blow out the pain. He pulled his knife from a pocket in his cargo shorts and handed it to her.

Beth tugged on the bottom of his shirt. "I'm about to ruin your t-shirt."

"Just cut my shirt, not me."

She cut the band from the bottom of his shirt, then cut a piece of cloth from her blouse. Beth put the cloth over his wound and used the strip of fabric from the t-shirt band to wrap around his arm. She tied the makeshift bandage tightly.

"That should stop any bleeding. Here's your knife." She placed it in his hand. "See, you can trust me."

But trust had been shattered when they left the cabin. Could one discussion put it all back together again? Maybe.

But only if they survived until they could have that discussion.

Splashing sounds from the river below.

"They're crossing. We need to hurry to that canyon."

Several bolts of lightning split the sky to the west.

"Good grief. Did you see that, Beth?"

"I saw the lightning."

"But the lightning was from several different clouds. They're just to the west and moving our way. It looked like a line of five or six huge CBs."

"CBs?"

"Cumulonimbus clouds. Thunderstorms. This is looking like the severe weather they have in the plains. I've never seen the atmosphere this unstable in Central Oregon."

"What does that mean for us, Drew?"

"It means we need to get off this ridge, now."

Chapter 23

"Beth, we need to get off this ridge, now." Why wasn't she moving? "Beth, lightning will be striking anything that sticks up. You know, like us. We could see large hail, microbursts, deluges, possibly even a tornado." He hooked Beth's waist. "Come on. I need to get you off this ridge."

She planted her feet and wouldn't move. "Drew, don't you have anything to say first?"

"Uh ... thanks for bandaging me up?"

"Getting a thank you from a beta male is like pulling—"

"Alpha male. But I already told you I don't fit the profile."

Was she trying to get some response from him that said the note was history? If so, was his lame 'thanks for bandaging me up' enough? Probably not.

"Drew, I ought to poke you in that wounded triceps. But, like you said, we need to get off this ridge."

Something had just changed in her. She sounded like the pre-argument Beth, the Beth he fell for in Texas.

"Let's run the deer trail to the top then go straight down the other side."

They cleared the ridge with no more shots fired.

With each lightning flash, Drew took a snapshot of the terrain ahead and adjusted their course. The vegetation had grown sparse and the flashes were frequent, allowing them to run down the ridge at near full speed.

Within a couple of minutes, they reached the mouth of the valley of pine trees.

Occasional bursts of gunfire now sounded in the distance, coming from the other side of the ridge. Not the burping of AK-47s, more of a staccato cracking like—it was Steve's M4.

Steve must be at the river, harassing Suarez from behind. In the process, he was buying Drew and Beth more time by making it harder for Suarez's men to advance. But this was a brief reprieve, because, eventually, they would fire at Steve to cover the gunmen who would advance.

Steve was one of the elite warfighters, most capable on the planet based on both training and experience. Drew must trust that Steve would be okay, and Drew must focus on saving Beth.

Regardless, the chase had not ended.

For several minutes, Beth and Drew climbed up the sloping valley, working their way through the pines.

Beth tugged on his arm. "Take a look at the ridge behind us."

Flashlight beams bounced wildly as Suarez's army topped the ridge and hurried down it to the mouth of the valley.

"How does he keep guessing correctly? We might have turned south or north."

"Drew, we've been going steadily westward since we left the place where ... where they—"

"Yeah. The place I carried you out of." A place that held terrible memories for Beth.

Her arms circled his neck and she clung to him. Finally, tears came. She needed to cry out all the terror from that horror-filled hour she'd spent in captivity.

She also needed to let go of her guilt about leaving that note. Maybe the arms around his neck were her way of doing that.

But Suarez had gained on them.

As much as Drew wanted to hold her and wipe away her tears, there was no more time for crying or consoling.

Flashlight beams appeared through the trees only a quarter-mile behind them.

While he held Beth, the night grew pitch black.

Either the lightning had stopped, or something was blocking it from view.

"Beth, I've got a really bad feeling about this."

"About me?"

"No." He cupped her cheek. "Not about you. About what's going on up there." He pointed upward. "Have you noticed how dark and quiet it's gotten? I think Suarez must have noticed too. The lights aren't moving in the lower end of the valley."

Beth curled an arm around his waist and turned toward Suarez's position. "What do you think is happening?"

"That moisture and unstable air from the east—the activity we saw earlier near Prineville—has made it here. The push from the Pacific is undercutting it, and we're about to see the roof blow off the tropopause."

"I thought you said the lid would blow off. Is there a difference?"

He blew out a sharp sigh. "I think there is a supercell overhead right now."

"Does that mean the atmosphere's about to supersize a thunderstorm?"

"Yeah. Any time now."

"What should we do?"

"If we stay here, Suarez will reach us and—"

"Then we can't stay here."

"But if we go higher up the valley, near the top of the ridge, the chance of that supercell unloading on us gets worse."

Beth touched her arm and then her cheeks. She put one hand on her hair. "This feels weird. I feel weird. My hair feels weird, like it's—"

"Beth, it's standing up. Crouch near the ground, but don't touch it." He pulled Beth down to his crouching position.

The strong electrostatic charge sent a tingling sensation over Drew's head and down his arms. "Lightning's going to hit something around here, really soon."

"Something like us?"

"I don't know. Lightning is unpredictable."

He looked to the east, down toward the mouth of the valley.

The lights of Suarez's men were moving again, maybe only three-hundred yards away.

"We've got no choice, Beth. They've closed on us. We need to run for the split rock at the upper end of the valley."

A blinding lightning bolt struck something in the lower end of the valley. The sound of the thunder was strange, almost like a growl instead of a rumble or a crack.

He tried to recall the material about severe thunderstorms his professor had covered in Meteorology 101. Lightning behaved strangely inside a vortex in a supercell. Maybe that accounted for the strange sound.

A tree exploded into flame. Another and then another burst into flame until a line of burning trees blocked the entrance to the valley.

He'd been worried about tornadoes or microbursts, but this could be far worse. Drew stood mesmerized by the powerful, destructive forces being unleashed.

"Drew? Drew?" How long had she been pulling on his shirt?

"I'm coming. Race you to the split rock." Drew took off up the valley holding her hand.

"You're not funny, Drew West."

He stopped less than a minute later, when the back of his neck became hot. The area around them lit up with bright yellow light. Drew turned toward the fire.

Beth turned with him and stared at the flames. She pressed one hand over her heart. "May God, help us."

"Maybe He just did. Either that or He has some hellish plans for taking us home."

Beth clung to him as they watched flames shooting upward, spinning, swirling, two- or three-hundred feet into the air.

The forest had become a tinderbox this summer, but it had gotten a lot more than the tiny spark it needed to set it afire.

The flames appeared to reach out toward them, as tree after tree burst into flames.

The downrush from the thunderstorm to the east of them had begun. It may not be a microburst, but when the air hit the ground, gale-force winds blew westward.

A hot blast hit Drew in the face. He turned away.

"Beth, this a strong downrush from the thunderstorm. It's going to push the fire toward us at forty or fifty miles-per-hour. Run for the rocks and don't stop for anything."

She glanced his way. "It will get Suarez before it gets us, won't it?"

"I don't know, Beth. There's no way to know." But it would probably cut Steve off. That would keep him safe after he completed his job.

Drew clung to Beth's hand as they sprinted up the valley, their way lit by the inferno.

The rock cliff came into view one-hundred yards ahead. Then a wall of smoke hit them, nearly knocking Drew off his feet. The scorching hot air enveloped them, smothering Drew and filling the upper end of the valley.

Beth coughed and gasped, then coughed some more. "I can't breathe, Drew."

"Don't stop. Just a little further." The back of Drew's neck stung from the fire's radiant heat. As much as he wanted to, he couldn't look back. He had to protect his eyes from the hot, dry blast hitting his back.

How much further? He didn't know, because now he couldn't see anything. Couldn't breathe.

Drew's coughing started. It became incessant.

Beth fell to the ground beside him.

She would die if he didn't get her out of the smoke and heat soon.

He scooped her up in his arms but stumbled as he tried to run.

Drew's strength had drained far beyond what physical exertion could account for. Maybe the explosive nature of the fire left the air oxygen-depleted. The smoke also stole oxygen from Drew's body as smoke filled his lungs.

Beth's raspy breathing sounds, like an asthmatic, were audible above the noise of the fire.

He'd heard that five minutes of smoke inhalation could kill a person. If so, he'd already used up a minute of his time.

Drew willed himself to keep moving forward, but he had slowed to a clumsy walk. The ground at his feet was visible from the intense light, but ahead of him ... nothing but smoke.

Maybe the fire had jumped ahead of them, spread by the wind that ripped at his clothing and blew Beth's hair.

Inside the valley, the wind had been blowing away from the fire. That gave him an idea and a small measure of hope. He could navigate by that wind.

Using Beth's hair, blown by the gale, as a compass, Drew moved with the wind. Moving away from the fire would also be moving up the valley toward the rock.

He drew deeper breaths to satisfy the craving for oxygen. That only brought deeper coughs. His coughs truncated each breath, giving him less air and a greater desire for oxygen—an endless cycle of choking that would soon kill him.

His back seemed sunburned. The bare skin on his neck felt like it had been baked.

The burning deep inside in his chest became as intense as the stinging on his neck.

Drew's feet dragged the ground with each step. He had to keep going for Beth, but he had no strength left.

Help me, please. Beth doesn't deserve any of this.

A sudden impact knocked him to the ground. He tried to stand with Beth in his arms but didn't have the strength.

Drew shook his head to overcome the stunned feeling. When he did, blood trickled down his forehead and clouded the vision in his right eye.

The realization hit him that he had cracked his head on the rock. Drew had reached the upper end of the valley.

Now he needed to find the opening that led to the crack in the rock.

The narrow passage through the rock promontory lay somewhere to the right of the center of the valley. Hopefully, he had run directly up the center as he followed the wind.

From somewhere deep inside, Drew found the strength to stand. He slung Beth over his back in a fireman's carry and slid along the rock to his right.

Dizziness almost sent him to the ground. He stopped and coughed. Then choked and fell forward to the ground.

But he hadn't hit the rock. He'd fallen into an opening.

Hope sent what little adrenaline was left in him coursing through his body.

He pulled Beth to the domino-like slab that hid the split in the rock. He dragged her around it and pulled her into the crevice. Cool air rushed in from the other side of the mountain, evidently drawn in by the updraft created by the fire.

Drew stood and sucked in fresh air. His first attempts were shallow breaths that ended in coughing spasms and intense pain in his lungs.

He coughed up the crud from his lungs and gradually his breaths became deeper, more satisfying.

Drew dropped to the ground beside Beth. She struggled to breath and appeared to be unconscious.

What had they said in his first aid course about treating smoke inhalation? His brain was still too foggy to recall. Mouth-to-mouth was the only thing that made sense.

He stretched her out on the ground, tilted her head back and opened her mouth to open her airway. Drew took a breath, pressed his lips to hers, and breathed out until her chest rose.

Beth coughed hard. That became a coughing spasm, with short gasps between coughs.

Still coughing hard, Beth reached for him.

"Breathe in then cough it out. Try to breathe in as much as you can before you cough."

Over the next minute, Beth's breathing grew deeper and the coughing more productive. Her lungs were clearing.

Drew sat, leaned against the rock wall, and listened to the fire. Its roar echoed through the crack in the rock with the sound of a jet engine.

Mixed with the sounds of the fire were other noises.

Drew focused his hearing on the higher frequency sounds.

They grew in intensity. Terrible sounds. Human sounds. Screaming and shrill shrieking from mouths that no longer sounded human.

Beth crawled beside him and put her hands over her ears.

Suarez and his men had been trapped in the box canyon that had become a literal hell on earth.

The evidence said justice would be served on Hector Suarez this night. As much as cartel murderers deserved it, hearing them die was gruesome and ghastly. Drew was glad Beth had chosen not to listen.

That Beth had covered her ears confirmed one of the reasons he held her in such high regard. She wanted justice, not vengeance. Distinguishing between the two was not something Drew was good at. Maybe Beth could help him, if her feelings about him hadn't changed.

The person who had brought Drew and Beth together, Suarez, became the person keeping them from what they most wanted, time together to let their relationship grow. Maybe they would now get that time.

From what Drew had seen, there was no way any of Suarez's men who had pursued them into the canyon could escape from the fire, except through the cleft in the rock. Drew had only found it with God's help.

Steve would have been on the east side of the fire. He could retreat to safety. He also had the Deschutes River for protection if he needed it.

Those who were dying in the canyon—Drew wasn't their judge, but it seemed just to him that the inferno should serve as a preview of their coming judgment. They were evil, murderers of women and children. And they had killed Beth's family.

Suarez and his cartel goons were getting what they had given to innocent people, a terrible death.

But what if one of those men, insane from the torment, stumbled into the crack and reached them? The thought jarred him.

He rose to his feet. "Beth, can you walk?"

No reply.

"I need you to try to stand. The passageway is too narrow for me to carry you."

"They ... might ... find us Drew. Help me walk." She struggled to stand, made it to her feet and stopped. "What's happening out there?"

"Sounds like Jonathan Edwards is preaching that sermon again and those sinners are in the hands of an angry God. If I remember correctly, he said God's enemies are like dry stubble before devouring flames, and it's easy for God to cast them into Hell."

"I wish it were easier to keep us out of it."

"Are you talking about what we just came through or Jesus and his sacrifice?"

"Drew, I can't even think, let alone make profound statements." She struggled to her knees.

He lifted her to her feet. "Let me hold you upright. Try to walk. Because, Beth, we need to get out of here."

* * *

Suarez slowed and turned his head toward the fire. He quickly turned back and continued his pursuit of the girl. Was he chasing the girl or being chased by the flames?

In an instant, the sky exploded into light bringing the brightness of noon to the valley filled with pine trees. The radiant heat hit the back of Suarez's neck leaving his skin stinging.

One of his men ran beside him now. "*El Capitan*, it is like the flames of Hell."

"Manuel, there is no such thing as Hell." Not for Hector Suarez. Only for superstitious peons.

Manuel cried out as a tree, only fifty yards behind them, exploded into flame. "I fear you are wrong, *El Capitan*." Manuel tripped on a dead bush and fell to the ground.

Words poured out of the man's mouth now. "*Dios te salve, Maria. Llena eres de gracia* ... "

Useless words of prayer.

Suarez ran into a rock wall. He couldn't climb it, and he was inside a box canyon, trapped on three sides with the fire closing in on the fourth side. He could flee no further.

Was there no way to make it to the ridge to safety?

I am El Capitan. I refuse to die like this. It will not happen.

The row of trees nearest to him detonated. The flames scorched his skin.

Suarez covered his eyes with his hands. Brighter than the sun, the light came through the flesh in his hands, through his eyelids, and it reached his eyes.

The burning of his flesh intensified.

Suarez fought back against it. He would not surrender to the fire.

"There is no Hell!" As he yelled the words, images scrolled through his mind's eye. A town in flames. Bodies burning, leaving the air filled with the odor of death.

It was hell for those people, and now it is your turn.

He had not spoken those words. They been spoken to him.

The tree beside him exploded into flame with a loud whoosh.

Noooo!" Suarez cried out his protest in a long, rebellious yell, until it involuntarily morphed to a scream when the fire enveloped him.

* * *

Drew held Beth's shoulders and guided her out of the crack in the rock. They emerged into an area of cool, clean air on the west side of the peak.

The glow of the fire lit the ridge above them and provided enough light to see what Drew needed to see, Beth's face.

He laid a hand on her shoulder. "Let's stop to catch our breath and to make sure no one survived by finding this passage. I've still got my Governor if we need it."

Beth turned and put her arms around his neck.

"Ouch. My neck feels like it's sunburned."

"I'm sorry, Drew." She hung her head. "I'm sorry for a lot of things. What I said—I'm a liar. Can you ever forgive me for that?"

"Didn't you tell a lie another time and then regretted it?" It was a low blow. He shouldn't have said that.

Tears overflowed one eye, then the other. Now, she had two streams flowing down her cheeks. She raised her hands toward him, then pulled them back and shook her head.

"Three words, Beth. Forgiving you would be the easiest thing in the world to do if I heard those three words."

She wiped her cheeks. "I forgive you is only three words too. It sounds like an even trade. But ..."

"It's that INTJ girl thing, right?"

"It's hard for me to say things that I feel. And I'm terrible at it. It's something you'll just have to get used to."

"Are you saying you'll give me the chance to get used to it?"

"Yes. If you still want me. I've thought about spending my life with you since that moment when you took Suarez down at the canyon, disarmed him, and saved my life. You should have known that."

"How could I? Most of the time you play your emotional cards pretty close to your, uh ... chest." He paused. "I forgive you, Beth. Will you forgive me for being so stubborn when it comes to certain things like—"

"You mean things like beating the tar—or do you call it beating the living crud—out of someone to protect the people you love?"

"There are some other words for it but, yeah, that's what I mean. You made a point of telling me how much you disapproved of—"

"My point was that I didn't want you to get yourself killed. I couldn't have just stood there and let you do that."

"Right. You couldn't have just stood there, so you were going to shoot me in the leg, so I couldn't stand there either."

"But I didn't, did I?"

"I called your bluff, so you threw down your gun and tried to use a pen instead."

"Can we forget that ever happened?" She took his hands in hers. "Please? I'll never lie to you again."

"Is that a promise?"

"Yes. But I may try to manipulate you on occasion."

"Like you're doing right now?"

"Drew, I've noticed there are times you don't mind being manipulated. Like after pillow fights." The first smile in hours turned the corners of her mouth upward.

"You'd never know it to hear us talking, but there's a deadly wildfire on the other side of this peak. To make sure we're safe, we should go down to the creek below. If the fire jumps the peak and reaches the creek, at least we'll have the water to protect us."

"Water sounds good. I could wash the smoke off me."

"And I've got burns that cold water would soothe."

The night grew darker the farther they walked from the ridge and the fire.

"Drew, I think it's raining."

By the time they reached the creek, a light rain fell.

"The big thunderstorm is dying. This won't last long. The heavy showers are probably to the east of us. This little bit of rain isn't enough to douse the big fire, but it might stop its westward progress."

"Fire or no fire, I'm getting in the creek. I want this smoke out of my clothes and out of my hair."

"That's okay as long as *you* don't get out of your clothes."

"I don't intend to, Mr. West."

"Good. Then I'll join you. The back of my neck is screaming, 'don't touch me.'"

"You need aloe vera."

"It doesn't grow around here."

"Yes it does. Aloe vera has been domesticated. I'll bet your mom has some in her kitchen window. But, Drew ..."

He lowered his scorched neck into the water. At first, it felt like ice, then it felt heavenly. "Yeah."

"When can we check on the horses?"

It wasn't a good idea. "We need to get back to the ranch to check on Steve. If Preston made his calls, or catches wind of what's going down out here, the ranch could be full of police cars. Maybe FBI too."

"You didn't answer my question. On our way to the ranch, won't we be going by where we left the horses?"

"Beth, we need to circle the fire well to the south, then go back along—"

"But that's still close to where we left Sundown and Dusty."

"You sure you want to do that?"

"I am. And I have another question."

"What's that?"

"Do you think any of Suarez's men survived?"

"As nearly as I could tell, all of Suarez's men that Steve didn't shoot were chasing us. They all came into the canyon, the fire trapped them, and incinerated or cremated them."

"That's a gruesome way to put it."

"Well, intense forest fires can reach temperatures of nearly fifteen-hundred degrees Fahrenheit. That's the temperature they use for cremation. Now I've got a question for you."

"I thought we were done discussing the note."

He nodded. "But, Beth, do you realize that tonight you finished your father's work?"

188

She didn't reply.

Drew waited.

"I—I didn't have much to do with finishing it. That was God using Steve ... and you. I did try to finish something else though, and—"

"And that was something that didn't need to be finished, because it was only starting."

She dipped her head. "Yes. It was only starting. But, Drew, can we please start by checking on the horses?"

Chapter 24

Beth's stomach churned worse than it had when Suarez tormented her with that hideous snake. A shiver shook her shoulders and she moved close to Drew's side as they walked up the steep hill toward the cabin.

Over the past hour, Drew had led her to rapids, well south of the fire, and they had waded across the Deschutes. Then they walked down to Steelhead Falls, where he got his rifle.

Most of the thunderstorms had moved away to the east. Stars filled the sky directly above them. The cabin came into view up the hill, a silhouette against the late-night sky.

On the horizon, to the south, a distant thunderstorm still flashed its anger at the intruding monsoon air. Or was it anger at the maritime air from the west? Drew, the Meteorologist, would have to make that discrimination.

Thinking about the weather, where they had walked, even thinking about the snake, kept her mind from going where it insisted on going, to the horses. Had Suarez slaughtered them like he did the people in Laguna? Had he shot both horses?

Maybe one had run away at the first sound of gunfire. "Drew, would the horses run away at the sound of a gunshot?"

"No, Beth. They were trained to stand still, so we could use them for hunting in the backcountry."

Then there was no hope. If Suarez saw both horses, both would be dead. Way West Ranch without Sundown wouldn't be the same.

There was no reason to ask Drew further questions about the horses, and continuing to speculate would only drive Beth crazy. She had to wait and let her stomach continue to—

Beth dropped Drew's hand and ran to a small bush, where she lost whatever remained of last evening's dinner at the cabin.

When she came back to the small path they'd been walking on, Drew took her hand. "My thoughts exactly. One thing we know, Suarez won't be harming any other living things, human or animal." He paused. "Beth, our packs are in the cabin. They're heavier than I feel like carrying right now, but we could get something to eat."

"Water. I just need some water."

They each took a bottle of water from the cabin and left to cross the ridge. From there, they would walk down to the old homestead fence, where they had left Dusty and Sundown.

"We can go back later and get our packs."

"But not on the horses."

"Have you ever ridden on an ATV, Beth?" Evidently, Drew didn't want to talk about the horses.

"We had ATVs in Mexico for riding in the desert. But it wasn't always safe to go out there, so I didn't ride."

"Then you're in for a treat."

"I'd rather ride Sundown."

"It's not far now. Who knows, maybe you can ride Sundown."

The tone of his voice wasn't convincing. She glanced up at Drew's face but couldn't read the silhouette against the night sky.

The old fence stood about twenty-five yards ahead and the irrigation ditch created a dark line paralleling the fence. This was the place, but where were the horses?

"Here are our saddles." Drew gave them a quick inspection. "They look okay."

"But saddles aren't much use without—" What was the dark form ahead on the ground? She wanted to look, but fear of what she would see stopped her.

Beth pressed her cheek into Drew's shoulder and looked away toward the ridge as they moved forward. If it was one of the horses, she didn't want that picture burned into her memory like those images from Laguna.

"It's Dusty. Beth, it looks like he's moving." Drew ran ahead and knelt beside the horse. "Take it easy boy. I'm just looking."

She watched from a distance, allowing the darkness to obscure any details.

Drew stood and circled Dusty, slowly, bending over to look several times. "It's okay, Beth. Come here and I'll show you what I found."

"Is he going to be okay?"

"I think so. There's only one wound. A bullet entered the back of his left shoulder and came out the front of the shoulder. Don't think it hit any bones. He must have been running away from them when they shot."

"Drew, does that mean the horses knew the danger and—"

"I'm not sure what it means for the horses. Maybe they sensed the men were bad. Dusty's wound doesn't look like it penetrated anything but the shoulder muscle. But he might not want to flex that muscle until we get a vet out here with some pain meds."

"Can we do anything for him?"

"Maybe. I'm going back to the cabin and get our first-aid kit. Here. Take my rifle just in case you need it."

She took the .30-30 from him.

"I'll run. Be back in ten minutes."

"Be careful, please."

"You too. Keep your eyes peeled, just in case. And don't shoot Steve if he shows up." Drew turned and trotted back toward the cabin.

Beth knelt by Dusty's head.

He sniffed her hand and recognized it.

She stroked his head and decided she wouldn't go looking for Sundown until Drew came back. She needed him beside her if things turned out the way she—

A whinny sounded in the distance, far down the fence line.

The sound of a galloping horse grew louder.

Beth stood, drew a sharp breath, and waited.

The big horse slowed and trotted up to her. Sundown neighed softly, snorted, and ran her cool, wet muzzle over Beth's outstretched hand.

She blinked back tears and patted the horse's head. "I don't have any treats for you ... wait. Drew's saddle."

Beth ran the fifty yards back to where they'd left their saddles, knelt, and opened Drew's saddlebag. She fished through it, until she felt a paper pouch, and pulled it out.

When she opened the pouch, Sundown's head moved over her shoulder. The big horse sniffed then whinnied.

"You've got to share, girl. But here." She dropped a sugar cube into her palm. It disappeared before she could stand.

"Come on. Let's see if Dusty feels up to having a treat."

Sundown followed Beth, the horse's muzzle nuzzling Beth's shoulder all the way back to Dusty.

Dusty wasn't interested in sugar until Sundown started begging for it. He raised his head, took one, and laid his head down again.

Five sugar cubes later, Drew's trotting footsteps sounded on the path.

He stopped about twenty-five yards away and watched Beth and Sundown. "Looks like I've got some competition."

"Yes. Stiff competition."

"I can see. Her muzzle's glued to your shoulder. What did you do, break into my stash of horsenip?"

"I treated her. I treated them both."

"Dusty ate some too?"

"Yes."

"That's a good sign." Drew walked her way and stopped beside her. "How is Sundown?"

"She ran to meet me, whinnying all the way."

"Then I think we should saddle her up and ride double back to the ranch, so I can call a vet. First, I need to rub some antibiotic on Dusty's wound."

"Did you put some of that on your arm?

"Used the mirror and got it covered as much as I could."

Drew knelt and gently covered the entry and exit wounds with antibiotic ointment.

"Drew ... do you think we still have a ranch?"

"Yeah. Suarez wanted *us*, Beth." Drew stood. "He wanted us so badly that he risked bringing forty men and their illegal weapons into the US. He wouldn't stop to destroy the ranch if that meant giving us more time to get away."

"You're probably right. I hope so."

As Drew saddled up Sundown, Dusty tried to stand. Evidently, he didn't want to be left behind.

Drew motioned toward the saddle laying loosely on Sundown's back.

Beth took over saddling Sundown.

Drew calmed Dusty. "It's okay, boy. We don't want you to start bleeding. We're coming back."

Dusty laid down.

Beth gave him another sugar cube.

By the time she finished, Drew had climbed into the saddle and lowered a hand to pull Beth up behind him.

"That's not how it's going to be, Mr. West. You're on *my* horse. Climb down and I'll help *you* sit behind *me*."

"We're not married yet so, technically, this is still *my* horse."

"You talk like our marriage is, how do the judges say it, settled law?"

Drew climbed out of the saddle. "We survived last night, didn't we?"

"Yes."

"Then I rest my case."

Beth mounted Sundown. "Resting your case only means the jury is out."

After Drew mounted the horse behind Beth, he wrapped his arms tightly around her waist and rested his chin on her shoulder. "This arrangement definitely does have some advantages."

"Do you know what my father would say if he were here?"

"Uh ..."

"You are *demasiado íntimo*."

"I get it. You don't have to translate. But the general idea is, keep your hands off my daughter."

"That's a loose translation." She leaned her head against his. "But Papa isn't here, Drew." It was the first time, since her encounter with Suarez, that Beth had been able to say that without fighting off tears.

"Beth, I don't have stirrups or a saddle. I've got to hold onto something."

"I guess you do, don't you?"

Drew's bear hug around her tightened.

After what she'd been through last night, the comfort of Drew's arms was exactly what Beth Sanchez needed.

In a few minutes, they reached the back road into the ranch and, in another quarter of a mile, they would be able to see the ranch house.

"What do you think we'll see at the ranch?"

"Based on my last phone conversation with Agent Preston, I'd be surprised if we didn't see a lot of police cars."

"After the night we had, that's comforting."

"Beth, sitting behind you, on your favorite horse, riding home without a Suarez in the world ... that's comforting."

"But there is a Suarez. Ricardo and a Grand Jury trial are waiting for us in Pecos."

"Leave it to an INTJ, like Beth Sanchez, to make things uncomfortable."

"Would you really want life with me to be boring?"

"Was that a hypothetical life with you or a hypothetical boring?"

"I don't think I should answer that ... yet. Changing the subject ..."

"You always do."

"What are the odds that Steve made it out safely last night?"

"Well, I can say this ... his odds are a whole lot better than ours were. Besides, didn't you once tell me that odds don't matter when God is involved?"

She nodded. "And He *was* involved."

Sundown picked up her walking pace. Probably sensing that home and the barn, with something a lot better than grass, awaited her.

"Did you learn anything tonight, Drew?"

"Probably a dozen things. Are you thinking about one thing in particular? Like God saying that vengeance is His, not mine?"

Was that a lucky guess, or—no. Once again, Drew knew. "Does that mean you won't be whacking every young punk who makes you mad?"

"Only when I need to defend someone. But, Beth, if anybody tries to hurt someone I love, I'll beat the tar, the living crud—whatever they need beaten out of them to protect the people I care about."

"The reason I'm asking is—"

"Is you want to know if your necessary and sufficient conditions have been met so that you can say yes to my question."

"Is that really how you think of me? Cold and calculating?"

"I'd say cool and calculating ... most of the time ... except after pillow fights. Then you're—"

"You've answered my question."

"But I've got more to say on the subject."

"Isn't there something authors try to avoid, something called overwriting? You know, when they say the same thing over and over in slightly different ways, until their readers just—"

"Got it. My answer was both necessary and sufficient. Subject closed."

They rounded a turn and looked for the ranch house. In the pre-dawn twilight, it was barely visible through the sea of red and blue flashing lights.

The lights reflecting off her skin turned her arms purple.

"Police. I guess Mr. West isn't surprised."

"He's not surprised at all."

"Not surprised? Drew, the day is just beginning."

"And what's that supposed to mean?"

"Anything ... or nothing." She smiled and turned her head toward him but couldn't focus her eyes on his purple face six inches from hers.

"You know, Beth, that smile, when you tell me stuff like that ... it doesn't tell me a thing."

"By the time you see it, I've already been told everything I need to know."

"Yeah. Right. But you, Beth Sanchez, have a crippling, information-sharing disability. You hog all the important stuff and nobody else gets to know it, especially if it's about you.

"No comment."

When they were about a hundred yards from the cars, a powerful beam of light blinded Beth.

Sundown stopped and snorted.

Beth looked away from the lights and urged Sundown on.

Drew buried his face in her hair. "I think the world just turned red and blue ... or maybe purple."

"It's them." A voice came from somewhere near the police cars. It sounded like Steve.

"Steve's safe," Drew said. "Prepare for the onslaught."

"Let me talk to them first." A tall, slender man in a suit approached them.

Sundown stopped.

The man reached a hand out to Drew. "Special Agent Preston. It's good to see you again, West." He turned to Beth. "And you too, Ms. Sanchez. Can you give me the nutshell version of what happened out there and the current status of the cartel gunmen?"

"Got some urns?" Drew slid down from Sundown's back.

"Some what?"

Beth climbed down from the saddle. "Urns, Agent Preston. Most of the men, including Suarez, are dead and cremated. Maybe ten or fifteen others are dead or dying from bullet wounds inflicted by Steve Bancroft."

"You three took them all out? And cremated them already?"

A man with a deputy sheriff's badge stopped beside Preston. "You can't cremate without a license. It could get you arrested."

The man either had a dry sense of humor, or he was trying to be obnoxious. "Tell that to God, Deputy, uh ... I can't read your badge," Beth said.

"Yeah, Deputy I-can't-read-your-badge. That's who you need to talk to about the forest fire that trapped and burned about twenty-five cartel members, including Hector Suarez." Drew chuckled.

"Well, I'll be—"

"No, Preston. You don't want to be that. We're pretty sure that's what Suarez got. But it's possible that one or two of the guys Steve shot are out there wounded. For all the others, you'll be either collecting bodies or ashes. The fire crowned and ran them up into a box canyon, where Beth and I led them. We heard them as the fire got them. It was gruesome."

"So you were in the box canyon and you survived, but they're all cremated?"

"Yeah. In a situation like that, who you know makes a big difference. If you don't believe in God, you might call them coincidences. But a strange combination of events led me to the split rock that leads out of the canyon to the other side of the ridge. We breathed a lot of smoke but got out through that crack in the rock."

The deputy kicked the dirt a few times with his boot then looked up at Agent Preston. "We'll search for survivors and bodies in the morning. The fire is probably dying down some, due to the rain. But it's still too much of a danger to approach it until daylight. Also, any survivors, hidden by the darkness, could start shooting at the police."

"I don't think you'll find any survivors." Steve had walked up to where they stood. "I shot fifteen of them. Probably killed ten outright. The able-bodied men chased Drew and Beth and were cut off by the fire. I was looking down from a ridge to the east when it crowned. Looked like Hell on earth. Flames leapt up three-hundred feet or more.

Whole trees exploded from the heat. The explosions split the air and cracked like lightning. The fire ran faster than a man can run."

"Good to see you in one piece, decoy." Drew gave Steve a hand. Then they went through some male ritual with their hands and arms that Beth didn't understand and didn't think the men did either. It stopped when Steve bumped Drew's upper arm.

"Ouch."

Steve grabbed Drew's shoulder well above the wound. "You got hit, bro. We need a medic to dress that and close it up."

"Yeah. I wouldn't want to have an infected arm on my wedding day."

"Izzat right?" Steve turned toward Beth.

Beth waited until Drew looked her way. "Drew West is full of it."

"We all know that, Beth," Steve said. "But, about a certain wedding, are you denying it or not?"

"She doesn't work that way, Steve," Drew said. "When she says something, it implies two or three other things which, if taken together, might answer your question. But you're supposed to know that without being told. She's an INTJ female. You gotta' read them in between the lines."

"Bro, I know what 'Drew West is full of it' means. There's nothing in between the lines. But it didn't answer my question about a wedding."

"Can we talk about something else, something more relevant," Beth said. She wasn't ready to reveal what was happening in her heart and mind to anyone else ... not yet.

"Yeah. Steve, call my mom at your place and have her call her vet. Dusty got hit in the shoulder by an AK-47 bullet and needs some pain meds and his wound treated. Just tell her he's along the fence by the old homestead."

"Hit once?"

"Yeah."

"Is it safe down there?"

"Yeah. If the vet comes in from the south, on the old homestead road, he'll be safe."

"You got it, bro. We'll talk about the other stuff later."

Preston blasted out a sigh. "Now that we've gotten all that out of the way, back to FBI business."

"And DEA business." Another man in a suit approached.

"Yes. And DEA business," Preston said. "Based on what Mr. Bancroft and you two described, I think we can say the fire wiped out the Del Rio cartel. And half of the Tijuana cartel."

"No. God wiped them out. Burned them just like they did to my town," Beth said.

Preston turned toward Beth. "Your father was Rafael Sanchez, wasn't he?"

Beth nodded. "After almost eight years, maybe there is justice on this earth."

Agent Preston dipped his head. "And Suarez didn't have to wait for a white throne for his judgment."

"No, sir," Steve pulled his cell from his ear and shoved it in his pocket. "Suarez thought he was his own god, *El Capitan* of his own soul. But the God who answers by fire— He is God. It was almost like Elijah and the prophets of Baal. Fire came down from heaven, a big bolt of lightning, and burned up everything."

"Well said, Ranger Bancroft." Preston grinned at Steve.

Steve cocked his head. "Don't I know you from somewhere?"

"You didn't *know* me, but you sure gave me a hard look when you passed by my SMAW while you were reciting the Ranger's Creed."

"You were there that day eight years ago?"

"The day your outfit saved America—you bet I was," Preston said.

"Did you hear that, Drew?" Steve turned toward Drew. "Hey, bro. Did you hear that?"

Drew looked Steve's way. "Go away for a few minutes. I'm busy." He turned back to Beth and took both of her hands.

"Marry me, Beth. I have a contract for what will be my breakout novel. I need a business manager."

"That didn't work the last time you tried it, Drew. What makes you think it will this time?"

"Because I love you the way you are, Beth Sanchez. I don't have anything to prove to you. And an imperfect man, one you know everything about, is asking you."

Drew dropped to one knee on the ground.

Beth leaned back against the police car and stared at him. How was he going to do this? He wasn't going traditional on her, was he? And he didn't have a ring.

Steve turned around, looked at them, and scratched his head.

Drew jumped up, ran to Sundown and fiddled with her saddle. He trotted back and took a knee.

"Give me your sexy, swollen ankle, Beth."

"Here it is. But it's not swollen. It's just a little sore from running on it. As for sexy … do you have an ankle fetish, Drew?"

Steve pointed at Drew. "Bro, this isn't manly, and it's not how it's done."

"Butt out, Ranger Bancroft. This is my battle." He looked up at Beth. "Do you want me to tell you what I was really thinking when I held your ankle by the Rio Grande?"

"Are you actually going to admit that in front of this audience?"

Now four policemen had joined Steve watching the marriage proposal that threatened to become a train wreck.

"Yeah. I am. I was thinking that I wanted to take care of you for the rest of my life."

"That's what you said last time, Drew. I don't like reruns."

"But you'd better not give me the same answer, because then I wouldn't have to take care of you for very long."

"Was that a threat? You really know how to scare a woman." She felt anything but threatened, but Drew needed to deduce things like that on his own.

"Beth, despite our earlier conversation, for you and me, real life can be better than a Nicholas Sparks romance."

"I certainly hope so. Half the time, somebody dies, and the other person's left behind, crying their eyes out ... along with all the readers."

"Just say you'll marry me. You can live here, ride horses whenever you want. You can manage my writing business and Way West Ranch too. You'll be the CEO of two companies. And you can bring Mom into the twenty-first century."

"When?"

"When what?"

"When are we getting married?"

"Is that a yes?"

The crowd had grown to at least fifteen policemen and a policewoman.

"I want to marry a man who is decisive. When are we getting married, Drew West? How long does it take around here to get—what do the cowboys say, hitched?"

"I think it takes at least three days for—"

"Okay. Three days."

"Like, for real? Three days?" His voice had cracked on three.

"Take it before I change my mind."

A policeman tapped Drew on the shoulder. "Take it, dude. If you don't, I will."

"Okay. Three days."

"So in three days I get two jobs and a horse ranch?" She extracted her ankle, reached out a hand, and pulled Drew to his feet.

"That's about the size of it."

"It's bribery. Pure and simple."

"But you're forgetting something, Beth?"

"What?"

"I know for a fact that you're one of those INTJ women, the rarest type on the planet—sarcastic, never show affection, or much emotion. But at some point—don't you have something you want to say to me?"

She cupped his cheeks. "I love you too, Drew West." There. She had said the words and now it was time to show him.

Beth leaned closer to kiss Drew, but he held her by the shoulders, then he took her left hand. Drew lifted it up where the flashing blue and red lights turned it purple, just before he slipped something over her ring finger.

She wiggled her fingers. It was big and wasn't exactly round, but it was familiar looking. "A D-ring from Sundown's saddle?"

"I can get something more suitable tomorrow."

"For now, this is perfect." She kissed Drew.

She had initiated all three of their kisses. But this one was much longer than the first two. Maybe it was time to test her theory. In the middle of the kiss, she concentrated on the strategy she had used to capture Drew.

I've closed the drawbridge. You've been trapped inside the castle. You thought you had stormed it, but I caught you, and now you're mine, Drew West.

Beth continued her betrothal kiss. She ignored the audience, ignored her fear of emotional exposure, ignored everything except the man who had saved her life more times than she could count, the man who offered her more than a romance writer could ever give a woman.

Speaking of writers, Drew was one. And she still didn't even know what he wrote, yet she had promised to marry him.

What if he wrote horror? That could be changed. After all, she would be his business manager, his wife, and she was an INTJ. If he wrote horror, that's what his life would be until he changed genres.

As she finished the kiss, their audience clapped and whistled.

But Drew cocked his head and gave her the strangest look. "Beth, I want to marry you more than I've ever wanted anything on this planet. But I should have realized that when you opened the drawbridge you were setting a trap for me, weren't you?"

He had done it again. Drew knew. "I opened the gate because I wanted you inside, and I closed it to keep you. The only question was, would I have to open it again to kick you out?"

"Are you always strategizing, planning, and analyzing things in that INTJ mind of yours?"

"How else can a person know if they're right?"

"Beth, all's right that ends right."

"Are you trying to quote Shakespeare to me? Don't answer that. Just tell me this ... did *we* end right, Drew?"

"I don't know. We've only just begun."

There were other people around them. How could she have completely forgotten that? One of them approached her and Drew walking at a snappy pace. Agent Preston.

"I've got some news for you two. You get to honeymoon in Pecos, Texas. They're about to convene the grand jury."

Beth gave the FBI agent a serious frown. "It seems there's always a Suarez messing up my life."

"But, Beth, aren't you glad we turned down witness protection?" Drew draped an arm over her shoulders.

"Yes. But it is a bit like marriage."

"Witness protection?"

She nodded. "Once you take it, there's no turning back."

Epilogue

Drew stood in the living room of their cottage at the Lajitas Golf Resort and Spa, studying his wife. They had chosen the location for its proximity to Big Bend National Park. But there was no golfing on their agenda.

"A honeymoon in Texas isn't a bad thing, Drew." Beth cinched up the laces of her hiking boots. "I didn't get to finish my Big Bend hiking excursion. But this time we get to go by ourselves."

Beth stood and sauntered across the living room. "The last time we were by ourselves here, bad things happened."

Wearing shorts and a tank top, Beth was in a class by herself. She could walk onto the stage at the Miss Universe Pageant and steal the show.

"What do you mean by bad things happened?"

"I sprained my ankle."

Half of the time she was the great minimizer, the other half was all hyperbole or sarcasm. "So you don't think Suarez showing up was a bad thing?"

"Drew, Suarez ... *isn't*. That's all we need to say about him."

"And when the money for his lawyer ended with the death of the Del Rio Cartel, Ricardo's lawyer lost interest."

"He more than lost interest, Drew. The man disappeared, forcing Ricardo to take the best plea bargain he could get."

"Which means that you and I won't be coming back for a trial. The indictments by the grand jury scared poor Ricardo into making that plea bargain."

"And that means we need to make the most of our time here in Big Bend. Who knows when we'll be back here. So let's get going. Santa Elena Canyon awaits."

"Let's wait a few minutes, Beth."

She slipped her arms around his neck and gave him a seductive smile. "What are you proposing, Mr. West?"

"Just that I'd like to get to the Canyon around 8:00 a.m."

Beth stepped back and shook her head. "It's still August. We need to start early. It's going to be hot on the trail." She studied his eyes for a moment, then stepped into his arms again.

"It's hot in this room." Had he said that or just thought it?

"Drew, are all men like you?"

"What do you mean?"

"Your thoughts are well, shocking. Like a lot of things that go through men's minds."

She was good at remembering his words and using them against him.

Drew reached for a couch pillow.

Beth tackled him.

She knocked him back onto the couch.

It was a picture-perfect tackle—shoulder into his stomach, arms clamped together like steel bars. She even drove through him like Drew's old coach had taught his players.

Where had she learned that? Watching American football on the weekends?

She landed on top of him. "Remember what happened the last time we had a pillow fight?" Her eyes darted playfully around on his face until her gaze locked on a spot a little south of his nose. "If I kiss you, will you take me to the canyon now?"

"What time is it?"

"How can you think about time at a time like this?"

"Evidently, you can. You just said, 'a time like this'."

"Fine. Then you can't kiss me until we reach the Canyon."

"Fine. I can wait."

Beth made him wait.

Forty-five minutes later, Drew drove their rental car into the parking lot near the canyon.

With packs on their backs, they walked hand-in-hand from the trailhead to the place where they had sat beside the Rio Grande. In those magic moments, they had made the kind of connection that lasts a lifetime.

Drew glanced at his watch and nodded.

"What, Drew?"

"Nothing."

"No. Last time it was nothing. This time it's ..." She leaned toward him to give him the kiss she'd made him wait for.

A raft emerged from the canyon.

She sucked in a breath and pulled Drew down into the bushes by the river.

Another raft floated out of the shadows.

Then a third.

"We need to get out of here." Beth whispered. "You didn't bring your Governor, did you?"

"No. Didn't think I'd need it."

"Look. Now there are four rafts."

"What should we do, Beth?"

"You're asking me? What happened to the Drew West I ran off to Oregon with?" She glanced at the river and gasped. "They're coming to our side, to the riverbank."

Drew unslung his pack and stood.

"No. Don't. Get down." Beth grabbed his belt and jerked downward. She almost pulled off his shorts.

"Hey, bro! Haven't seen you in a while."

It was a familiar voice. Hunter.

They rose out of the bushes and Beth stood nose-to-nose with Drew. "Delaying. Always looking at your watch. You set me up, Mr. West."

"Mrs. West, I'd never do a thing like that to my bride. She might have Whittaker prosecute me—maybe for trafficking in jokes on government land."

"No. For spousal abuse." She cocked her arm and focused on his shoulder. "I'm going to punch you so hard that you'll never—"

"Please don't. I just got the stitches out."

When she pulled her punch, Drew grabbed his pack and took off trotting down the trail for the canyon. "Catch you later, Hunter. Sometime after Beth catches me."

* * *

So Drew had a nice ending planned to this, after all the mischief. And he had recreated part of that moment when they first met.

Beth would catch him. They would kiss in the shadows of the canyon, and tonight Beth would lie under the stars with Drew beside her at a spot for which they'd obtained a camping permit.

Later, while sleeping under the stars, she would dream of horses, of foals frolicking in green pastures, of Mel and Coop, of Drew's mom, Mattie, who had made Beth her daughter. But mostly she would dream of the man she had given her heart to.

I'll go with you, Drew. Let's get out of here.

Those words had been a one-time decision, a commitment of her life. It was much like Beth's commitment to follow her Lord. That had been an act of her will to place her faith and trust in another, just as she had done by pledging her love to Drew.

Her pledge declared that Beth was all in, the kind of decision from which there's *no turning back.*

But then ... who would want to?
I'll go with you, Drew. Wherever He takes us.

The End

If you enjoyed *No Turning Back*, please consider leaving a rating and a brief review on Amazon. Reviews are difficult to get and greatly appreciated by authors and readers. You can find *No Turning Back* on H. L. Wegley's Amazon Author Page.

Author's Notes

In writing *No Turning Back*, the biggest challenge I faced was creating the character of my heroine, Beth Sanchez, such that she would be a high-priority target for the drug lord, Hector Suarez. My solution was to combine two real-world stories that I will share, briefly.

The first story is about the man who inspired the Mexican people to form militias to stand up to the oppression of the drug cartels.

A doctor in Mexico decided to take action to stop the bleeding of the local people caused by drug cartels' demands for monthly protection money. When the monthly payments became more than the people could pay, the doctor rallied the men of the community to form a militia. He armed and trained them, and systematically drove the cartel from the area.

Mexican law enforcement feared the cartels and many government officials were corrupt, often cooperating with the drug lords. The people preferred to risk their lives by forming a militia rather than depend on the unreliable government for protection.

Each time the militia defeated a group of cartel thugs, the doctor would confiscate their weapons and use them to grow his militia. As word of his success spread throughout the country, he would travel to new areas and preach about freedom from the cartels. The people heard the doctor's message, believed it, followed him, and drove the cartels from their areas.

After the doctor moved on, the militias he left behind continued to grow on their own, until their power became a concern to the Mexican government. By this time, the doctor had become a folk hero, a man who had killed a lot of drug cartel members. Consequently, he became the government's focus for solving its perceived militia problem.

The government's plan was to stop the doctor and then hope the militias would die.

The government arrested the doctor on illegal weapons charges. This was almost too ironic to believe. The doctor had done the job that Mexican law enforcement was afraid to do, and they arrested the man who could have shown them how to defeat the cartels and restore law to Mexico. But the officials were too afraid and/or too corrupt.

Law enforcement imprisoned the doctor for three years, until his influence diminished, then freed him in 2018 without ever trying him on the weapons charges. He's not as active as he once was, but still tries to inspire his countrymen to drive the cartels from their towns and villages.

The real-life doctor became Beth Sanchez's father, Rafael Sanchez, in my story. To complete Beth as a character, I needed to give her strong feelings of guilt. I used another real-life story to accomplish that.

While researching drug cartels in Mexico, I ran across a terrible incident, the Allende Massacre of 2011. It seems that the U.S. Drug Enforcement Agency (DEA) obtained some critical intelligence information about the leaders of Los Zetas, perhaps the most violent drug cartel in Mexico. Evidently, the DEA shared the intel with Mexican law enforcement, and a dirty cop, or other compromised official, told Los Zetas.

As a result, the cartel swept through Allende and the surrounding area, breaking into houses, looting, burning buildings, and killing people to ensure they found the Los Zetas traitors who leaked the information to the DEA. They killed hundreds of people in horrible ways.

No one was ever prosecuted, and the incident was hardly investigated due to fear of Los Zetas. To this day, the people of Allende suffer in silence.

I borrowed this incident and had my heroine lie to her mother to get permission to go with friends to a place her parents had forbidden her to go. When she returns, she finds her parents, and most of the people in the town, dead.

I laid a big guilt trip on Beth Sanchez. She lied and lived, when a good daughter would have stayed home and died. That provided the wound in her backstory, her character flaw, and it set up the black moment for her in my novel.

It was a nasty thing to do to a beautiful young woman like Beth, but authors have to make a living somehow, and pain in the backstory is one way we do it.

Another problem arose in the scenes that comprise the final conflict, that big battle where the hero and heroine save the day or save their lives.

I ended up with my hero, Drew, pitted against thirty cartel thugs who were armed with AK-47s. Drew needed some help to defeat the cartel members or the story would not have been credible. In short, I needed a skilled warfighter to help Drew. So I borrowed Steve Bancroft, Army Ranger and weapons specialist, from *Voice of Freedom*, which is set in the same area as *No Turning Back*. Steve lives only a few miles from Drew's horse ranch.

A little about the setting for *No Turning Back*—the story starts in Big Bend National Park. While my wife and I lived in Texas, we intended to visit the park, but we never did. I've driven through West Texas, a little north of Big Bend, so I'm familiar with the area around Fort Stockton and Pecos, the location of the Federal District Court for West Texas. But, unfortunately, I had to visit the park virtually.

I know the Central Oregon setting well, because my wife and I spend a week there every summer. My photo collection contains over 13 GB of digital shots that I've taken from Sun River, Bend, Sisters, Crooked River Ranch, and northward to Lake Billy Chinook, and Madras.

I shot the desert scene used for the background of the cover. On the printed version, the scene wraps around to the back. I took this picture in the twilight following a sunset at Crooked River Ranch. Smoke from forest fires turned the sky an eerie mixture of reds, purples and shades of gray.

The setting for the horse ranch in *No Turning Back* is near the Deschutes River, a short distance from Steelhead Falls, and a little east of the town of Sisters—beautiful country. I mention the Three Sisters in the story. These three, adjacent volcanic peaks grace the western skyline from the ranch's location.

Although there is no horse ranch at the exact location I chose, there are several ranches in the area that breed and sell thoroughbred quarter horses, equine dragsters, as Drew called them. They are the fastest horses in the world, for short distances. Quarter horses are featured in movies, rodeos, and they are the preferred horses for ranch work.

Several times in the story I mention Beth's personality type, INTJ. I gave Beth that personality because it is surrounded by a lot of mystique. The Meyers-Briggs Type, INTJ, denotes introverts who use their intuition combined with rational thinking. They can often jump from a small amount of information to a conclusion that explains, with incredible accuracy, all the observations and how they relate to human origin, meaning, destiny—sorry. I got a bit carried away. However, INTJs are called the Research Scientist type and sometimes the Mastermind, for good reason.

The rarest personality on planet Earth is the female INTJ. Comprising 0.8% of the population, this type is queried on the Internet more than any other personality type. Why? Because of the mystique surrounding them and the difficulty in establishing a relationship with them. It's a real challenge to win their trust, thus their love. But once a person does, they have a loyal friend or, if they're lucky, a spouse for a lifetime.

Nearly all INTJs are highly intelligent. They don't display a lot of emotion—unless you consider sarcasm an emotion—though they feel things deeply. For this reason, some people call them insensitive. To get an INTJ to say, "I love you," is difficult. Drew experiences that with Beth. But once an INTJ says it, they mean it and will stick with you when no one else will. That's who I wanted Beth Sanchez to be, a heart worth winning. I hope you like her and her story.

If you enjoyed *No Turning Back*, please consider leaving a rating and a brief review on Amazon and possibly Goodreads. Reviews are hard to come by and greatly appreciated by authors.

My next release, *Virtuality*, is a stand-alone story—a high-stakes, techno-thriller with romance. It's a clean, character-driven story featuring equal parts romance and suspense. Look for it in November 2018.

H. L. Wegley

Don't miss H. L. Wegley's award-winning, political-thriller series, with romance, *Against All Enemies*:

Book 1: Voice in the Wilderness

Book 2: Voice of Freedom

Book 3: Chasing Freedom (The Prequel)

Read all three books in the *Witness Protection Series*—action and romance with thriller-level stakes—clean reads that are never graphic, gratuitous, or gross.

No True Justice

Can witness protection be used as a political weapon? Someone in the DOJ thinks so. And if the political weapon fails, there are other choices.
One way or another, Gemma Saint is a saint someone thinks should be a martyr.

Witness Protection Series

Book 1: No Safe Place

Book 2: No True Justice

Book 3: No Turning Back

Romantic suspense with thriller-level stakes
Vince van Gordon inherits control of break-through, virtual-reality technology that could make him one of the wealthiest and most powerful people on the planet. But, if commercialized, the technology would likely shred the fabric of American society beyond mending. Keeping it a secret only delays the inevitable. And, once the secret is leaked, there are people who will kill for the wealth and power. Stopping it may literally require an Act of Congress, and Vince will need the help of brilliant Jess Jamison, his childhood soulmate, the girl who shattered his heart seven years ago.

Releasing November 2018

58222529R00136

Made in the USA
Columbia, SC
18 May 2019